P9-BZM-953

"I don't have a single person I can call for help..."

"You could just say yes."

Maddie hesitated. Her *youngie* did not.

Clapping, her son popped his head through the window. "Yes, please!"

Smiling past her frustration, Maddie graciously gave in. "Okay. You've talked me into it. I appreciate the offer." Pride shattering, relief lightened her worry.

"Then it's settled."

Abram returned her flashlight. For the first time in a long time, he didn't think twice about his face. Maddie had neither asked about his scars nor even acknowledged their presence. That alone gave him hope. Like a seed awakening after a long winter's slumber, he felt a sense of renewal deep in his spirit. Was it possible *Gott* was guiding him in a new direction?

He didn't yet have that answer.

But I want to find out...

Like the Amish, **Pamela Desmond Wright** is a fan of the simple life. Her childhood includes memories of the olden days: old-fashioned oil lamps, cooking over an authentic wood-burning stove and making popcorn over a fire at her grandparents' cabin. The authentic log cabin Pamela grew up playing in can be viewed at the Muleshoe Heritage Center in Muleshoe, Texas, which was donated to the city after the death of her grandparents.

Books by Pamela Desmond Wright

Love Inspired

The Cowboy's Amish Haven
Finding Her Amish Home

Visit the Author Profile page at LoveInspired.com.

Finding Her Amish Home

Pamela Desmond Wright

If you purchased this book without a cover you should be aware that this book is stolen property. It was reported as "unsold and destroyed" to the publisher, and neither the author nor the publisher has received any payment for this "stripped book."

Recycling programs for this product may not exist in your area.

ISBN-13: 978-1-335-58585-1

Finding Her Amish Home

Copyright © 2022 by Kimberly Fried

All rights reserved. No part of this book may be used or reproduced in any manner whatsoever without written permission except in the case of brief quotations embodied in critical articles and reviews.

This is a work of fiction. Names, characters, places and incidents are either the product of the author's imagination or are used fictitiously. Any resemblance to actual persons, living or dead, businesses, companies, events or locales is entirely coincidental.

For questions and comments about the quality of this book, please contact us at CustomerService@Harlequin.com.

Love Inspired
22 Adelaide St. West, 41st Floor
Toronto, Ontario M5H 4E3, Canada
www.LoveInspired.com

Printed in U.S.A.

For with God nothing shall be impossible.
—*Luke* 1:37

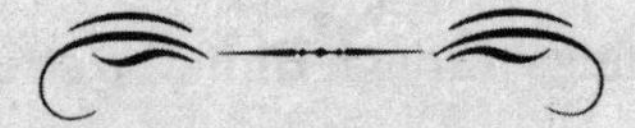

This book is dedicated to all the people who said
"you can't."
Yes, I can.
And I did.
I can do all things through Him who strengthens me.

Special thanks to my editor, Melissa Endlich,
and my agent, Tamela Murray.
They lift me up when I am down.
They make me look a lot smarter than I really am.
And they had enough faith in my abilities
to give me a chance.

Chapter One

Inhaling the scent of freshly baked bread, Maddie Baum pressed a hand to her middle. Her stomach rumbled, reminding her lunchtime had come and gone. She'd been so busy unpacking that she'd forgotten to eat breakfast.

"Would you like to try this *brot*?"

Maddie glanced at the girl working behind the counter. Perhaps seventeen, the young lady was clad in a plain but crisply ironed dress. A clean white apron was tied around her waist, her long hair was neatly plaited and tucked beneath a prim white *kapp*, and a few bobby pins held everything in place.

"Oh, it looks fabulous."

"*Ja*," the girl agreed in a softly accented voice. "Please, try." Knife in hand, she cut a generous slice off an unwrapped loaf. Adding a smear of strawberry preserves, she offered the sample. "You will enjoy."

Biting into the treat, Maddie savored the crispness of the crust and the sweet-tart fruit.

Swallowing, she smiled with approval. "Delicious."

The clerk beamed. "Delivered to the market this morning. And the *bewahrt* is also homemade."

She cocked her head, inwardly translating the foreign words. Unlike many *Englischers*, she had a familiarity with the language the girl spoke, having learned at the knee of her grandfather. *Opa* always spoke to his *enkelkinder* in the *Deitsch* language, taking care to make sure they understood and respected their unique heritage.

Finishing the bite, Maddie brushed the crumbs off her fingertips. "Tell them both it is *gut*, the best I've ever tasted."

Cheeks reddening, the teenager shyly dropped her gaze. "May I wrap one for you?" she asked, slipping a large round loaf into a paper wrapper. She also added a jar of preserves.

"You talked me into it." Maddie accepted her offerings, adding them to the selection in her basket. Mentally totaling what she'd spent, she glanced down. Panic immediately stopped her cold. Her seven-year-old nephew, at her side just a moment ago, had vanished.

Anxiety shredded her. Even though she'd told Josh to stay nearby, he was nowhere to be seen. A thousand what-ifs invaded her mind. She immediately gave herself a mental kick. How could she have lost sight of him? She'd only taken her eyes off him for a few seconds.

This wasn't the first time Josh hadn't minded. He had a willful streak. It didn't help that he was probably restless. Days of packing and driving hundreds of miles to an unfamiliar destination was enough to make any kid eager to run and explore a strange new place.

The clerk noticed her distress. "Are you unwell?"

"The boy who was with me," she explained. "He's wandered away."

"The little *braunhaarig* child?"

"Yes. The brown-haired boy."

The clerk pointed. "I saw him walking that way."

Given a direction, Maddie nodded gratefully. "*Danke.*"

Lips pulled into a thin line, she wove her way around other shoppers milling through the aisles. Adding haste to her steps, she doubled back to the dessert aisle. Earlier, Josh had made a fuss when she'd said no to a cake with fudge icing. Looking into his eager face, she'd gently reminded him sugar was not allowed except as a special treat. Of course, he didn't understand. Already a hyperactive youngster, Josh was prone to tantrums when he didn't get his way. His reaction was typical—sticking out his bottom lip in a pout and dragging his feet.

Sure enough, she located him.

Two men—one elderly and bearded and the other younger and clean shaven—had the boy bracketed between them. Both were clad in white shirts, plain pants and work boots, which clearly identified them both as Amish. Other shoppers eyed the trio, pretending not to notice the commotion in their midst.

The look on the older man's face warned all onlookers that he wasn't pleased. Leaning heavily against his cane, he waggled an angry finger in the air. "The *boi* is a *dieb*, a thief," he spat, speaking loud enough for all to hear. "I want him arrested."

Rubbing his fingers against his temples, the younger fellow gave the old man an indulgent nod. "I hear what you're saying, Gran'pa," he returned, speaking in a softer, calmer voice. "But I can't very well go calling the police on a *youngie*. Maybe we need to find his parents first."

Walking on numb legs, she interrupted the

duo. "Excuse me. I'm Maddie Baum, and you seem to be holding my runaway child."

The younger man greeted her with a serious expression. "Glad you're here, ma'am," he said, adjusting the frames of black-rimmed glasses. "I'm Abram Mueller, and this is my *grooss-daadi* Amos."

Gaze pinging from the old man's frown to Josh's puffy face, Maddie struggled to keep her composure. "What's happened?"

The old man thumped his cane on the ground. "The *boi* has stolen from me," he said. "Have ye not taught the child thou shalt not steal?"

Tears rolled down Josh's cheeks. "I'm sorry. Please, don't let them call the cops to take me to jail!" His voice, wobbly and panicked, revealed his fear.

Reaching out, she pulled her nephew into a tight embrace. Josh trembled, terrified at what he imagined jail might be.

"*Entschuldigen Sie, mein Herr,*" she said, stroking his hair to soothe his anxiety. "I am truly sorry for what he's done."

Both men looked surprised.

"*Du sprichst Deitsch?*" Abram asked.

Dipping back her head, Maddie gazed into brown eyes dotted with flecks of gold. Her breath caught. The clerk was a handsome fellow, and it was hard not to look twice. Black curls ruled over his strong brow and straight nose. Slim and trim, he wore his clothes well. One side of his face was scarred, but that didn't detract from his looks.

Tamping down the rise of attraction, she cleared her throat. "*Ja*," she answered. "I mean, yes. Some of my *familie* were born in Pennsylvania."

Abram smiled. "I'm impressed."

A huff of exasperation slipped past her lips. "I'm not impressed you caught Josh stealing." She turned to the old man. "What did he take? Whatever it is, I will pay for it."

Shaking his head, Amos Mueller grunted. "*Bäckerschokolade*," he answered, pointing to a shelf of neatly wrapped bars. "Put them down the front of his trousers."

Maddie eyed the unsweetened squares of baker's chocolate. Josh had obviously mistaken them for regular candy bars.

Kneeling, she took him by the shoulders. "Didn't I tell you no sugar?"

Sniffing, Josh rubbed his runny nose with the back of one hand. "Yes."

Maddie put on her sternest look. "When I say no, I mean it." Standing up, she guided him around to face his accusers. "You will apologize to your elder for taking something that did not belong to you."

Gulping down a mouthful of air, Josh drew back thin shoulders. "I'm sorry. I didn't mean to do anything wrong."

Refusing to budge an inch, Amos's nostrils flared. "*Ach*, a *boi* your age should know better," he scolded. "'Tis a sin to steal."

Abram stepped in. "And to forgive others their trespasses is divine."

"That's not in the good book," the cranky old man grumbled.

"Then I'll go by what *is*," Abram countered. "Something about *judge not lest ye be judged*."

"I suppose the good Lord knows what He is talking about," the old man conceded.

Shaking his head, Abram clucked his tongue. "Everyone makes mistakes, and everyone deserves a second chance. We're all only human." He gave Josh a stern frown. "As for you, young man, I'll let your mother school you in *Gott*'s commandments."

Maddie breathed a sigh. Relief lessened the grip of anxiety. "*Danke*. I'll certainly do that. Let me pay for our things, and we will be leaving."

"Sounds fair." Abram tipped his head. "Good day, ma'am." He strode away, returning to his work in the busy market.

Amos huffed but said nothing more. Cane in hand, he hobbled away, muttering under his breath about the tongues of snakes.

Grateful for the reprieve, Maddie took a firm hold on Josh's hand. "I think we need to go."

Josh kept his gaze down as they walked. "Are you mad?"

"No. Not mad. Just disappointed. Why would you do that?"

He looked up, face pinched. "I was hoping you would say we could go home," he explained. "I miss my friends."

Emotion moistened Maddie's eyes. She blinked hard. *No, no. Keep it together.*

"I know you do," she said gently, giving his small hand a squeeze. "But give it time. You'll make new friends."

His grip went slack. "I just don't like it here. It's boring."

"We haven't been here very long. Give it time and we'll have a lot of things to do after we get settled in and I get a job."

Josh shifted from regret to recalcitrance. "I don't like it!" Clenching his fists, he stamped his feet.

She reminded herself to stay calm. Josh just had to keep pushing back. His behavior wasn't acceptable and other shoppers were, again, beginning to stare.

"That's it. I've had enough." Hand on his shoulder, she guided him toward the counter.

Head dropping, he dragged his feet. "I hate this place! I want to go home!"

Maddie mentally shook her head. Josh didn't know it, but they could never go back to Pennsylvania. Not now. It was too dangerous.

Lord, help me. Give me wisdom and strength.

The quick prayer buoyed her spirit.

"We're going. Now." She reached for her purse as they approached the counter. Bread, strawberry preserves, peanut butter, a whole baked chicken and a glass jar of milk brimming with real cream. For a healthy treat, she'd picked out several fat red apples.

Dipping inside her bag, she groped for her wallet.

Her hand found nothing.

A fresh rush of ice filled her veins.

Her wallet had her entire life inside—license, insurance cards and all the cash she had in the world.

But it wasn't there.

Abram Mueller wasn't the sort to take a second look at a woman. Still, something about Maddie Baum made him pause. Her image hovered at the forefront of his mind, refusing to be banished.

Intuition tapped him on the shoulder.

Turn around.

The fine hairs at the nape of his neck rose. The first thing he'd been taught as a child was to never ignore the still, small voice. As a man firmly committed to his faith, the one thing he never doubted was that *Gott* moved in mysterious ways.

His servants were obligated to obey.

"What are You telling me, Lord?"

Pivoting on his heel, he searched for and found Maddie and her son as they headed to the checkout stand.

With her blonde hair neatly plaited and pinned, her simple gray dress, light sweater and black flats weren't anything a fashionable *Englisch* woman would wear. Add a white *kapp* and apron and she would look like any proper Amish woman.

Knowing she was from Pennsylvania and that she spoke the *Deitsch* language led him to guess she was formerly a member of the community or at least closely associated through *familie* ties. Hard to tell if she was married or not. Amish women didn't wear wedding rings.

Abram watched as she casually dipped a hand into her purse and then stopped dead. Her head dropped as she dug frantically, obviously seeking something she couldn't locate. A moment later, she abandoned her basket and headed for the exit.

It didn't take a rocket scientist to interpret the scene.

Empty purse. No money.

One of his brothers claimed the basket abandoned on the check stand. Like most Amish, Abram was the product of a large family, with many siblings.

"*Ach*, the way people are," Samuel muttered under his breath.

Abram stepped up. "Hold up."

"What's going on?"

"The lady who left her groceries seems to have lost her wallet."

"The woman with the little *boi*?" Samuel asked.

Abram made a quick decision. He couldn't go home and sit down to a hot meal while others would go without. "I'll pay for her items," he said and reached into his pocket, fishing out a few bills. "This should cover what she got."

Handing over the money, he glanced toward the parking lot, hoping he had enough time to catch the pair before they departed.

Samuel visually totaled the items. Shaking his head, he refused the offering. "You know our policy," he chided gently, filling a recyclable bag with the groceries. "We will always feed the hungry."

"I know, but Gran'pa is on a tear today."

Samuel laughed. "He will get over it. He always does."

"*Danke.*" Grabbing the bag, Abram hurried into the parking lot. Craning his neck, he caught sight of Maddie.

Belting her son into the back seat of a beat-up blue station wagon, she yanked open the driver's-side door. Bending, she slid her hands into every nook and cranny between the seat and floor of the vehicle. The car she drove was an older model and had obviously seen better days.

Relieved she hadn't driven away, Abram doubled his steps. As the distance closed, he caught a few words of her worry.

"I know I had it. I know it."

Josh, trying to comfort her, reached out and touched her shoulder. "It's okay, Mom."

At the end of her tether, Maddie Baum snapped. "It's not okay!"

Her *youngie* immediately burst into tears.

Maddie burst into tears, too. "Oh, I'm sorry. I'm such an idiot." Unable to find the lost item, she lowered her head. Her slender shoulders trembled.

Abram walked up. "Excuse me. May I have a moment of your time?"

She immediately straightened. Her face paled. "Josh didn't steal anything else, if that's what you're thinking."

"That's not why I'm here." He held up the grocery bag. "I believe you forgot this."

Irritation gave way to a sad sigh. "I didn't forget." Her bravado seeped away. Hands lifting, she wiped under red-rimmed eyes. Uncertainty clouded her expression. "I seem to have misplaced my wallet. I haven't got a cent to pay you."

Abram shook his head. "That's not necessary." He held out the bag a second time. "Please."

Her jaw tightened. By the glint in her eyes, pride had bestowed upon her the stubbornness of a barnyard mule. "It wouldn't be right to take advantage."

"I don't expect to be paid. This is for you and your *sohn*. I couldn't let a mother and child go away hungry."

Her gaze drifted from the groceries to his face and back again. "You may not know it, but it's a blessing right now."

"The Lord says we shouldn't neglect to share what we have."

She accepted his offering. "I promise, I don't make it a habit of losing my money. I must have misplaced my wallet while I was unpacking. That's the last place I remember seeing it."

"So, you've just moved to Humble?"

"*Ja.* We haven't been here long."

Abram spread his hands. "Welcome to our town. I hope your *familie* will like it here."

A wistful smile shadowed her lips. "I think we will."

"There are a few Baums around here," he continued, looking for a reason to stretch the conversation out a few more minutes. "Might you be kin to any of them?"

Fine brows knitted. "Unless they settled here from Pennsylvania, I don't think so."

His gaze flared with inquiry. "Lancaster?"

Shaking her head, she hurried to clarify. "Somerset. Born and raised. It's the second-oldest Amish settlement in the state."

"I see. It's quite a long journey from Pennsylvania to Wisconsin. You're far away from your *familie*."

Swallowing visibly, Maddie blinked hard. Sadness lingered in the depths of her eyes. "There's nothing for us in Pennsylvania anymore—and hasn't been for a long time," she said quietly. "Except for Josh, I don't have many relatives."

Her reply piqued his curiosity. Through their brief conversation, she hadn't mentioned being married. "I'm sorry to hear that."

Clearing her throat, she angled her chin. "No, I apologize. I didn't mean to get so personal. That didn't come out the way I intended."

"No apology necessary." Getting up his nerve, he held out a hand. "I always like to say a stranger is just a friend waiting to be met."

She put out her hand. "I'm always glad to make a new friend."

Warmed by her acceptance, he smiled. "Me, too."

Though she appeared fragile, her grip was surprisingly firm and straightforward. A handshake revealed a lot about a person, and hers showed a woman determined to hold her ground.

The sound of a child's anxious voice interrupted. "Mom! Mom, can we go now?" Josh screwed up his face. "I'm hungry."

Maddie's hand slipped from his. "I'm sorry. I should get home." She pushed out a sigh. "Josh has been cranky all day."

Disappointment prodded. If he'd had his way, Abram would have liked to talk all day—about most anything—just to spend a few more minutes with her. It was the first time someone, especially a female someone, hadn't stared at his face.

Maddie looked him straight in the eyes and didn't flinch. When speaking, most people tended to talk at him but not to him. Their expressions were always the same—curiosity mixed with pity.

For most of his life, the scars had made him feel freakish. After a while, he'd learned to ignore the surreptitious glances. No reason to dwell on the damage or feel sorry for himself. Knowing he wasn't a handsome man, he tried to be a kind one.

"Settling into a new place is always hard. And Humble is quite a change from a bigger city. Can't say we have a lot of trouble here."

She brushed a few stray strands of hair off her forehead, tucking a loose wisp behind one ear. "That's what I was hoping for. A quiet place with no trouble."

"I think the last time someone called the police, it was to get a cat out of a tree."

Amusement lightened her features. "If that's all the crime you've got here, I'm impressed."

"Humble is a whole lot of nothing going nowhere. If you're looking for quiet, it's here."

One of the things that made the town such a tourist attraction was the horses *clip-clopping* down the tree-lined avenues made of cobblestone, easily blending in with gas-powered vehicles as people made their way around. Life was simple, unhurried. At 5:00 p.m. sharp, most every store closed. Come dusk, the Main Street sidewalks were empty.

"I'm afraid Josh is going to find it hard to adjust. He's upset about leaving his friends, though I can't say I'm sorry. Our neighborhood wasn't the best."

As the conversation was winding down, Abram

made one final attempt to keep it going just a little bit longer. "Our community sponsors summer activities every other Saturday evening in the park for the *youngies*. Perhaps you'd be interested in bringing your son to play."

Interest warred with conflict deep in her gaze. "Why, thank you. But we're not Amish."

"All are welcome. And the little ones aren't the only ones who need to socialize. After the games, we have a potluck meal. It gives us a chance to enjoy fellowship with our *Englisch* neighbors."

Her expression brightened. "It's been forever since I've been to an Amish potluck. Not since I was a kid."

"Most everything's homemade," he said, adding to the enticement. "If nothing else, everyone goes home with plenty of leftovers."

Clearly tempted, she nibbled her bottom lip. "It would be nice for Josh to make a few new friends before he starts school. He's feeling so out of place."

"The games start at six this evening," he said. "Horseshoe tossing, tug-of-war, kickball...a bit of everything."

Interest piqued, she asked, "Would I need to bring anything?"

"Just come ready to gab with the other ladies and have a good appetite."

A smile crinkled the corners of her eyes. "Thank you for inviting us. I've been praying I made the right decision to move to Humble."

Abram felt his insides knot. The sincerity of her words touched him deeply. With a gaze harboring shades of melancholy, Maddie Baum reminded him of a fine china figurine—shattered and then glued back together by clumsy, uncaring hands. Some pieces were still missing, but she'd somehow overcome the damages and become even more striking.

He dipped his head, peering over the rims of his black-framed glasses. "I believe *Gott* put us where He wants us to be. It might take time, and we might go astray, but eventually the Lord leads us all home."

Chapter Two

Warmed by Abram's words, Maddie basked in the hope and optimism he offered. "I appreciate the welcome you've given us."

Shuffling his feet, he stuffed his hands in his pockets. "Well, that's just my thoughts on the matter. You might think differently."

A brief surge of emotion tightened her throat. She'd grown up in a devoted household and had a good familiarity with the teachings of the Bible and how to live a decent life. "I don't," she said softly. "I've been trying to find my faith again."

He offered an encouraging nod. "*Gott* never gives up on anyone. All you have to do is surrender your will to His guidance, and He will provide."

"I'm doing my best." She stepped back, again offering her hand. "But I've taken enough of your time. Thank you again for your help and the kind welcome. I appreciate it."

Returning the gesture, he again clasped her hand between his larger ones. His touch was sincere and reassuring. "I hope to see you both later." Smiling, he gave Josh a quick wink. "And you, young man, be sure and mind your mother."

Josh's expression was somber. "I will."

Letting her hand drop, he turned and walked away. There was a confidence in his stride as he returned to mingle with customers browsing in the market.

Relieved that she'd found a social outlet for Josh, Maddie placed the groceries in the back seat before buckling him into his booster seat. The clock on the dash read ten after twelve. There was enough time to get home and finish unpacking.

Looking forward to a relaxing evening visiting with other parents, Maddie slipped behind the wheel. A twist of the ignition bought the engine stuttering to life. Painted a patchy blue and rusty in spots, the Chevy probably should have been retired at least a decade ago. Still, the engine ran, the brakes worked and the tires weren't too bad. The old vehicle tended to overheat in high temperatures, but if the radiator was full of water, it kept chugging down the road.

She was grateful to have it. Not only did it keep her mobile, but it had also given her the ability to pack up and leave Pennsylvania behind. After learning Josh's father was due to be released from prison, she'd decided it would be safer to disappear before he showed up on their doorstep.

Reaching up to adjust the rearview mirror, she caught a glimpse of her pale, pinched features. The last five years had taken their toll on her, mentally, physically and emotionally. And now, the man who'd caused all the angst in her life wanted custody of his son.

Fingers circling the steering wheel, Maddie felt the specter of panic rise in her chest. A tight, squeezing sensation wrapped itself around her lungs. A chilly grip seized her spine, digging sharp claws deep into the marrow of her bones. So warm a moment ago, she was suddenly freezing cold. The blood in her veins felt as frozen as an arctic glacier.

She'd learned that even if a person had a kind face, goodness wasn't always abundant in their hearts. Some people, cruel in spirit and black in their souls, set out to deliberately hurt others.

Cash Harper was a prime candidate.

Unbidden, his image reared up in her mind. He'd been everything her twin sister, Margaret, had believed she wanted in a boyfriend.

Good-looking. Puppy-brown eyes under a mop of hair that perfectly complemented his tanned physique. Despite the warning signs, Margaret had fallen head over heels in love with the *Englischer* before discovering Cash had a very dark side.

Liar. Bully. Thief. There wasn't an ounce of good in him, and he'd pushed her sister to the breaking point time and time again. When Margaret had finally had enough and tried to walk away from the relationship, Cash Harper had taken her life.

Brutally and without remorse.

Chest heaving, Maddie gulped in a mouthful of welcome air. Her vision misted, but she refused to let a single tear fall. She'd never thought she'd be on the run, hiding her nephew from the man who had ended her twin's life. Josh had been so young when his mother died that he believed *she* was his mother. She'd never had the heart to correct him. The truth would just be another burden on his small shoulders.

She hated the deception she'd created but felt it was necessary. As far as she was concerned, Cash had lost his parental rights when he'd killed her sister. After he was put behind bars, she'd promised herself that she'd keep him from ever getting custody of Josh.

"Are you okay, Mom?"

Blinking hard, Maddie nodded. "I'm fine, honey." She swiped at her eyes. "Sometimes I just get sad."

"I'm sorry I made you mad."

"I'm not mad. I'm just disappointed. We've talked about you taking things that aren't yours. Stealing is wrong, and you have to stop."

Shame clouded his features a second time. "I won't do it again," he promised, crossing his heart. "I'll be good."

Maddie reached back through the gap in the seats to give his hand a reassuring squeeze. It was their own secret signal, one she and her sister used to share when they were growing up. It meant everything was going to be okay.

"I'm going to hold you to your word, sport."

"Sure." His tone held no enthusiasm, only resignation.

"It'll get better. I promise."

"I guess." Restless, he kicked at the passenger seat in front of him, scuffing it with his tennis shoe.

She forced a smile, injecting a bit of cheer into her voice. "Mr. Mueller has invited us to the community games this evening. Aren't you excited about meeting new people?"

Another shrug. "Not really." Turning his face away, Josh stared out the window.

Refusing to be discouraged, Maddie decided

to leave the subject alone. Shifting the car into Drive, she moved through the parking lot. A few minutes later, she turned into the street, following the traffic.

Putting her focus into her driving, she followed a twisty asphalt road, enjoying the pastoral beauty of the Wisconsin landscape. Fields thick with corn and other late-summer crops were broken up by trees and quaint houses with white fences. Signs placed in driveways advertised items for sale—fresh eggs, baked goods and vegetables, along with other handmade items. Humble was a popular tourist destination for those seeking out handmade products and homegrown produce.

Speeding wasn't an option. The horses and buggies sharing the road moved exceedingly slowly, clopping at a leisurely pace. With nary a sign of electrical wires and old-fashioned equipment in the fields, it was easy to imagine living life in past times. In Amish country, a simpler, gentler time was reflected in the landscape and the people who'd settled it.

Twenty minutes later, Maddie pulled into the driveway of the house where she'd rented a small attic loft. The neighborhood was an older one. Perched on a piece of property bracketed by trees and fencing covered with grapevines, a rambling three-story house sat like a jewel amid a lush green lawn and gardens. Painted white with blue trim, it was picture-perfect.

Safely parked, Maddie unbuckled Josh before claiming the groceries. Walking up the cobblestone path, she bypassed the front porch and headed around to the side entrance that would take them into the kitchen. The door was wide-open.

"We're here," she called, pausing to let Josh pull open the screen door.

Busy with her two-year-old grandchild, Wanetta Graff glanced up. "I hope you didn't have any trouble finding your way around," she said, settling the toddler into a highchair.

Maddie lifted the bag she carried. "Nope. Found the market and picked up a few things."

She frowned as Josh rushed past her. Rather than stopping to say hello, he ran up a narrow set of stairs leading to the third level.

Watching him go, she sighed. Josh wasn't happy with the small apartment, but the rent was reasonable and included laundry facilities. For an extra twenty dollars, Mrs. Graff would also look after Josh while Maddie searched for work.

"*Gut*." Giving the little girl a rattle, Wanetta returned to her baking, peeking inside the propane stove to check the sweet breads she baked from scratch every day. "You do know meals are provided with your rent. Just come down and eat."

"I know. But it seems like so much extra work for you."

Wanetta chuckled. "No extra work, dear. There's always room for a few more at the table." Slipping on a pair of heavy mitts, she opened the oven door and retrieved two pans. Spatula in hand, she transferred the pastries to a wire rack to cool.

"We'll be going out this evening. One of the shopkeepers said there is a community gathering in the park on Saturdays for the kids to play games."

Sliding another pan of cinnamon rolls into the oven, Wanetta wiped a hand across her brow. Clad in a crisply ironed dress, she had a white apron tied around her waist. Long hair threaded with gray strands was neatly tucked beneath a prim white *kapp*.

"*Ja*, that's so. You and Josh should have a fine time."

"I'm glad Mr. Mueller invited us. I'd worried there wouldn't be much for Josh to do."

"Let me guess. You must have talked to Abram. He's a *gut* man. I've known him since he was a little one. His *mamm* and I were friends."

"He was very kind and welcoming."

"Shame he's still unmarried," Wanetta continued matter-of-factly. "Lot of women just can't see past those scars."

"That's too bad." Truth be told, she hadn't really noticed his disfigurement. She'd been more taken with his gaze, so gentle and concerned, and his smile, which shone with sincerity.

A sudden clattering sound interrupted conversation.

"Oh, Jessa," Wanetta exclaimed with a laugh. "Have a care."

The sweet-faced little girl reached out for her toy. Dressed in a pair of pink footie pajamas, her wispy curls were askew. "G'amma," she cooed.

Maddie retrieved the toy. "Oh, she's such a darling."

Jessa's expression brightened, a grin splitting her face. "Ta," she said, giving her rattle a furious shake.

Wanetta covered her ears. "Looks like I'm going to have to listen to that thing all day."

Gazing at the pair, Maddie felt regret burrow deeper. When she was younger, she'd hoped to have a daughter of her own someday. But after watching her sister endure such terrible abuse in her relationship, she'd determined to steer clear of men.

Tucking away her private lament, she offered the pair a nod. "I should run these upstairs and check on Josh."

"Sounds fine, dear."

Leaving the pair behind, she trekked up the narrow stairs, entering a small antechamber at the top. Passing over the threshold, she stepped into the loft. Far from being dark and cramped, the attic space was bright, open and airy.

Setting the groceries on the counter, she glanced around. Her missing wallet sat on the kitchen table amid a few boxes yet to be unpacked.

Despite her somber mood, she smiled. For the time being, the loft was perfect for her and Josh. The living space had a kitchenette, a dining table and a couch that folded out into a bed. A second bed was behind a privacy screen, as were an armoire and a couple of cedar trunks for extra storage. A door near the rear of the attic concealed a small bathroom. Three bay windows facing the morning sun provided ample light and warmth. A lot of skill and craftsmanship had gone into the design.

The loft already felt comfortable—far different from the cramped low-income apartment they'd left behind. Its dingy, cracked walls, dated fixtures, a heater that barely worked and loud neighbors weren't the best, but it was all she could afford in Pennsylvania.

She glanced at Josh. He sat sprawled on the

couch with his tablet. Staring at a blank screen, frustration shadowed his features.

"What's the matter?"

He gave the electronic device an aggravated shake. "I can't make it work. Nothing will come on."

Maddie hesitated. One thing Josh would have to get used to while living in an Amish community was the lack of some modern conveniences, such as internet. Even though the Amish in Humble were up-to-date when it came to using propane or solar-powered appliances in their homes and businesses, the boardinghouse wasn't wired for any phone, television or internet services.

"There's no Wi-Fi here."

Josh's face crumpled. "But how am I going to watch my shows?"

"You're going to have to give them up for now."

Mouth setting into a tight line, Josh tightened his grip on his tablet. "That's not fair!" Hands flying over his head, he threw it across the room. When it struck the floor, the fragile glass and plastic shattered into pieces.

Appalled by his behavior, Maddie clenched her teeth. *Count to ten*, she reminded herself. *Don't lash out in anger.*

Closing the distance between them, she said, "You know that's not acceptable. You're going into time-out to think about what you've done." Grabbing a kitchen chair, she turned it to face a nearby corner and pointed. "Sit. Now!"

Clenching his fists, Josh poked out his bottom lip. "No!"

Maddie pointed again. "It's not up for discussion."

Face puffy and red, Josh slid off the couch. Stomping with every step, he threw himself into the chair. "I hate you! You're mean. And I hate this place!"

Feeling a twinge behind her eyes, Maddie rubbed her fingers against her temples. "You can sit there and cry all you want," she said, forcing patience into her voice. "Nothing's going to change."

Josh wailed louder.

Letting him bawl, Maddie headed to the bathroom. Shutting the door, she leaned against the narrow vanity. A glimpse of her pale reflection gave her pause. Never in a thousand years would she have dreamed she'd take on the care of a child that wasn't hers.

Emotion squeezed her heart. Of course, she'd had no choice. Her sister was gone, and there was no one else to raise Josh. She was doing the best she could. Nevertheless, she felt like a failure.

Oh, Lord. How do I do this on my own?

* * *

"You're awfully quiet today. Is something wrong?"

Giving his eldest brother a glance, Abram struggled to keep his expression neutral. "I've just got a few things on my mind, is all."

Flipping open the lid of a paper cup, Rolf took a quick sip. "Oh? And what might that be?"

Abram shyly brushed off the question. Since meeting Maddie Baum, he'd thought about nothing else. He'd spent the entire afternoon hoping she would accept his invitation. Now that work was done for the day, folks had begun to gather in the city park for a fun evening of games and socializing. People buzzed around, their voices filling the air as games were arranged.

Even though he'd searched the crowd time and time again, there was no sign of Maddie or her son.

He tamped down his disappointment. He felt silly he'd already confided in his younger sister, Lavinia. He'd told her everything. Rolf would get the details soon enough.

It was foolish of me to think she'd come. No sensible woman would accept a stranger's invitation, even if the event was open to the public.

Reluctant to admit what was really on his mind, he let a shrug roll off his shoulders. "Nothing really important. Just stuff."

Rolf shifted on the hard bench to make himself more comfortable. His ample belly jiggled. He took a bite of the doughnut he'd sneaked out the picnic basket his wife had packed.

"I see," he prompted between bites. "So, have you given any thought to asking Edith Albrecht to the church social next month?"

Abram kept his reply short, clipping off his words. "She said no."

Rolf's lips puckered. "Ah. That's too bad."

"It is what it is." No reason to show his disappointment. By now he was used to women turning him down. He didn't even know why he bothered.

To distract himself, he glanced around the park. Trees and neatly clipped hedges bordered the town's park and recreational area. Several men had commandeered the barbecue grills, preparing to grill the hamburgers and hot dogs everyone enjoyed. Soon the scent of sizzling meat would fill the air. To wash it all down, the women had prepared pitchers filled with icy sweet tea and tart lemonade.

Spreading a blanket in a shady spot, his younger sister, Lavinia, sat feeding her infant from a bottle. A few other *fraus* who also had *kinder* to care for visited with her. Gathered like hens, the women all enjoyed catching up on the week's gossip.

"Then ask another *fraulein*," Rolf urged before wiping a bit of Bavarian cream off the corner of his mouth. "A wife isn't just going to drop from the sky. You have court a woman."

Here it was again. *The talk.*

"I know what you're all expecting. You never let me forget it. But—"

"But what?"

Leaning forward, Abram propped his elbows on his knees and laced his fingers together. A painful sensation nipped at the bridge of his nose. "You might not have noticed, but women aren't exactly attracted to my face. And a lot of people still hold my past against me. Memories are long, and no one's forgotten what I did."

He certainly hadn't. Near twenty years had passed since he and his friends had set Old Man Zook's barn on fire.

Rolf's expression softened. "You were just ten when that happened. We all know it was an accident."

Abram tipped his head, showing his left profile. "Doesn't matter what the truth is. No woman wants a man with half a face."

Even as he said the words, his guts twisted into painful knots. He'd never forget the flames scorching his skin. He'd also never forget the devastation of seeing two of his friends perish.

The event haunted his every waking moment,

as did the guilt. Even though others had forgiven him, he couldn't forgive himself. Through the years, he'd spent many a sleepless night praying to the Lord to ease his burden. But the peace he sought continued to elude him.

Brow furrowing, a short burst of air escaped Rolf's nostrils. "The scars aren't as bad as you've made them out to be in your mind. And I know a lot of girls who would say yes if you asked them out. But you never do."

Abram pinned him under a stare. "Who?"

Rolf returned a straightforward gaze. "What about Alva Blek? I know you've always had a little bit of a crush on her."

Abram waved a hand to cut him off. "I heard Alva got engaged to Peter Stutz last week."

Rolf's brows lifted. "Well, I must have missed that news."

"She wasn't my type, anyway." He pretended disinterest. "Besides, I've got more than enough work to keep me busy."

"Methinks you doth protest too much." Eyes crinkling around the corners, Rolf looked at him levelly. "You're living, but you're not enjoying it."

Rather than argue, Abram shut down. He wasn't in the mood to argue. The subject never found any resolution, no matter how many times they discussed it.

"I'm fine. Really."

"Are you?"

Tiring of the conversation, Abram rubbed his fingers against his temple. "Can we not talk about it anymore?"

Conversation paused as an *Englisch* mother pushing a baby carriage strolled by. Her husband, proud as a peacock, strutted beside her, toting the heavy bag of essentials a newborn required on an outing.

"First *kind*," Rolf commented. "You can always tell."

Abram gave the couple a passing glance. Although he longed for a *familie* and *kinder* of his own, he doubted he'd ever be so blessed. Instead of having a wife who greeted him with a kiss, he awakened to an empty bed. Instead of cradling the sons he so dreamed of raising, he'd resigned himself to never knowing the joys of fatherhood.

"Rolf!" a voice called. "Will you get Hannah's teething ring out of the buggy?"

Abram glanced toward his sister-in-law. A slight woman with lovely brown hair and expressive eyes, Rolf's wife wrestled with her squirming child.

Rising from the bench, Rolf adjusted his shirt and striped suspenders. "Fatherhood calls," he said, and claimed his hat. "Looks like Violet needs help with the *kind*."

"Go tend to your *familie*."

Hat set firmly, Rolf started to walk away. Pausing, he pivoted on his heel.

"*Gott* has plans for you," he said presciently. "Plans to prosper, plans to give you hope and joy. And, yes, even a helpmate. The promise is there. Trust in the Lord, and He will bless you."

Abram felt uncomfortable under his knowing gaze. "*Danke, bruder.*"

"Just have faith." Going on his way, Rolf completed his errand and joined his wife.

Feeling lost and out of sorts, Abram gazed across the park.

Angled toward the horizon, the sun was beginning its slow descent. The air had cooled, shedding the oppressive heat of earlier.

A chorus of children's voices filled the air. "*Onkel* Abram, come play!"

He smiled at the *youngies* headed his way. The children piled on, smothering him with hugs.

"Will you join the game?" his nephew Zeke implored. Twins Hiram and Hershel hovered nearby, adding to the chorus of pleas.

Teary-eyed, Zeke's smaller brother tugged at his sleeve. "The boys won't let me kick the ball," little Eli pouted. "I need big man legs."

Abram's melancholy lifted. The children's sweet faces and innocent spirits never failed to inject fresh energy into his spirit. Zeke and Eli belonged to his sister Annalise and never failed to bring a smile to his face.

"Well, we'll have to do something about that." Standing, he swooped his youngest nephew up, setting him atop his shoulders with an easy display of strength. "Now you have some legs to do some real kicking and running."

Small hands holding tight, Eli squealed with delight.

Surrounded by laughing *kinder*, Abram headed into the game. As he walked toward the playing field, he realized he had many things to be thankful for. His *familie*. His health. His job. Truly, the Lord was generous and had treated him well. When he went home this evening, he would be sure and bend a knee in thanks.

I have so many blessings. It would be ungrateful to ask for more.

Chapter Three

"You can get glad the same way you got mad."

Head down, arms folded tightly across his chest, Josh sat in stony silence.

Maddie unbuckled her seat belt. "You can sit there and pout or you can enjoy the evening. Which do you want to do?"

Josh repeatedly kicked at the back of the passenger seat. "Nothing."

"Just stop it," she warned. "There's no reason to keep pouting. You're the one who broke the tablet. I haven't got the money to replace it, so you might as well get over it."

Josh crumbled into tears. "I'm sorry. I didn't mean to."

Maddie softened. "I understand you were mad, but you have to learn that breaking your things and shouting won't get you anywhere."

"Why can't you listen to me? I just want to go home!" he cried.

Struggling to keep her composure, Maddie felt icy fingers squeeze her lungs. "That's not going to happen. Our lives are here now. I know you don't understand why we had to leave, but trust me when I say I'm doing my best."

Josh sniffled but didn't argue. Slumping in his seat, all the fight seemed to have gone out of him. Locked in his own misery, he sat staring into nowhere.

Firm in her resolve, Maddie refused to let his tantrum ruin the evening. Getting out, she rounded the vehicle. Opening the rear passenger-side door, she freed Josh from his booster seat. "Now come on." She pointed to the group of people filling the park. "Let's try to have a pleasant time."

Josh slipped out of the car. "I don't know those kids," he groused, resuming his stormy expression. "I don't want to play with them."

Maddie sighed. Josh wouldn't be happy until he ground her down with his whining and complaints. The only thing she could do was ignore him and hope he wouldn't depress everyone else with his attitude.

Retrieving the platter of cinnamon rolls Wanetta had generously sent along, she straightened. "Then sit and watch. And at least try to be friendly if anyone talks to you. That's all I'm asking. Okay?"

Josh recrossed his arms, hunching to make himself smaller. "I don't care," he mumbled, kicking the gravel beneath his tennis shoes.

Pulling in a breath to strengthen her own nerve, Maddie followed the cobblestone walkway leading into the heart of the park. An oasis of thick grass and sturdy old trees was enhanced by the presence of a pond, which was spanned by a small walkway and filled with goldfish. Ducks and geese wandered in groups, honking for bites of food from the people at the picnic tables. Along with a play area filled with swings, slides and other toys, the park offered ample space for baseball and other games.

People in Amish and *Englisch*-style clothing milled throughout the area. The joyous shouts of children at play filled the air. The adults sat on benches or on blankets spread over the grass. Men tended to the food as the women looked after their infants and toddlers.

Feeling out of place, Maddie halted her steps. Facing such a large gathering was intimidating. She didn't know anyone, and the idea of walking into the group was overwhelming. Beside her, Josh dragged his feet. By the look on his face, he was scared, too.

Swallowing hard, she fought to tamp down her

anxiety. Looking for a familiar face, she searched the group for Abram Mueller. She didn't see him, but she did spot his grandfather Amos passing the time with a group of elderly men. Nearby, she saw a few more men and women who bore a resemblance to him. Children of all ages surrounded them, ranging from infants to gangly teenagers. Surely Abram would be nearby. Having enjoyed their chat earlier in the day, she hoped to see him again.

"Come on," she urged, attempting to keep aggravation out of her tone. "Let's say hello." Pulling back her shoulders and angling her chin, she walked toward the group. Less certain, Josh trailed in her wake.

A woman holding an infant greeted her. "You must be Maddie."

Surprise halted her steps. "*Ja*," she answered, switching to *Deitsch* without thinking twice. It just seemed more natural to converse in the language she was taught as a child. "But how do you know my name?"

The woman laughed. "Abram Mueller is my *bruder*. He told me all about you and your *boi*." Her smile widened. "I'm Lavinia, and this is my daughter, Sophie."

"*Danke*." Unsure what else to say, Maddie added, "I was hoping my *sohn* would have a chance to make some new friends."

Petite with dark eyes, the woman gave her a wry look. "When Abram told me he'd met a Pennsylvania Amish girl, I didn't believe him." She visually swept Maddie from head to foot. "But you're definitely one of us."

Maddie glanced down. To save money, she made her own clothes. She still used many of the dress patterns she'd gotten from her grandmother. The simple styles were easy to make and suited her busy lifestyle. Forsaking cosmetics and jewelry, she'd tucked her long hair in a bun under a scarf.

"*Ja*," she said, and then corrected, "I mean, *nay*. My grandparents were Amish, but my mother went *Englisch* and took me and my sister away from the community when we were *youngies*."

"Well, you can take the girl away from the Amish, but you can't take the Amish out of the girl. I'm glad your *familie* decided to settle in Humble." Lavinia looked past her shoulder. "Is your *ehmann* here?"

Her stomach knotted. "*Nay*. It's just me and my *boi*."

"I see." Lavinia's gaze settled on the platter of cinnamon rolls. "My, those look delicious. If you would like to set them on one of the tables, we'll be eating soon." Setting her cooing infant against one shoulder, she gestured for Maddie and Josh to follow her. "Come, let me introduce you to everyone."

Relieved, Maddie followed her into the group. Fortunately, most people were content to accept her answer about whether she was married without prying. Most believed her to be a widow or abandoned by the father of her child. It was easier to say nothing than to tell a lie. The deception she and Josh lived under already hurt her heart.

"Everyone, this is Maddie and her son, Josh," Lavinia announced. "They've just moved to Humble."

A chorus of welcome filled the air. Everyone smiled or gave a little wave of acknowledgment.

"So happy to have you," a woman greeted warmly. "I'm Annalise."

"*Ach*, I see you have a boy the age of my Henry," a woman introduced as Violet added. "I hope they will be friends."

Lavinia finished the introductions, reeling off names as she introduced each in turn. "There are a lot of us," she said when she'd finished. "And most of us have *kinder*, too, so it's quite a group."

Trying to keep track of all the names and faces was dizzying. Raised with a single sibling, Maddie couldn't imagine being a part of such a large family.

"And then there's Abram." Lavinia pointed toward the ball field. "He's playing kickball over there in the field."

Towering over the kids, Abram was easy to pick out. Overseeing the group, he laughed and clapped, encouraging the younger children whenever the ball came their way. Other games were in progress around them—horseshoe tossing, tetherball and an impromptu game of touch football for the older kids. Everyone was having a fine time.

Maddie glanced to Josh. Arms still crossed in a defensive manner, his expression was slowly changing to a look of longing as he watched the other children play.

"Go. Ask if you can join in."

Shutting down again, he shook his head. "I don't wanna."

Maddie was about to reply when Abram came dashing up. A couple of children trailed in his wake.

A grin spit his face from ear to ear. "I was hoping you would come."

An immediate spark sizzled through her. Tall and broad shouldered, Abram was all corded muscles. Stray curls peeked out from beneath his straw hat. Suddenly, her throat felt closed, blocked by the intense pounding of her heart.

Gathering her wits, she returned his smile. "Thank you for inviting us."

"I hope my *familie* hasn't been giving you a hard time. Lavinia will talk your ear off if given half a chance."

"Not at all. Everyone has been so welcoming."

Abram looked at Josh. "And how are you, young man?"

"I'm okay," he mumbled.

Abram pointed to the twin boys accompanying him. "These are my nephews Hershel and Hiram. We're looking for one more for the team. Would you like to play?"

Josh shook his head. "I don't know any of these games."

Maddie cringed. A city school with a concrete playground and barely a half hour of recess didn't offer much activity for the children. As he grew older, it was getting harder to keep Josh active and engaged. Most kids he knew sat around with a smartphone or tablet in their hands, glued to the screen.

Abram jerked a thumb toward the ball field. "Well, do you know how to kick a ball and run?"

Josh gave a wary nod. "I think so."

"That's what the team needs. A *boi* who can kick hard and run fast," Abram continued and clapped his hands in an encouraging manner. "Come. Try it."

Shedding a bit of his reserve, Josh looked askance to Maddie. "Can I?"

"Of course. Go have some fun."

"Come on," Hiram and Hershel said almost simultaneously. "We need someone to play third base." The boys turned and sprinted back to their game.

"We really could use you," Abram added. "We're getting our tails kicked by the other team. We sure could use a home run."

By now, Josh's interest was piqued. "I would like to try."

"Then come and show us all what you can do." Giving Maddie a wave, Abram guided the child to the ball field.

Barely daring to breathe, she watched as Abram explained how to play the game. Her flitting gaze took in every detail. A variant of baseball, kickball was easier for children too uncoordinated to use a wooden bat. All they had to do was kick the ball and run to the marked bases before someone tagged them out.

It didn't take long for Abram to get Josh into the game. Within minutes, he was actively involved. His stormy mood broken, he played with gusto.

Maddie released a pent-up sigh. At last, the burden of uncertainty had lifted.

Sidling up, Lavinia gave Maddie a tap with

her elbow. "My *bruder*, he's *gut* with the *youngies, ja*?"

It was true. Abram was right in the middle of the action.

Watching her nephew kick the ball and run to first base without getting tagged out, Maddie nodded. "He is. I'm surprised he got Josh to play. I thought I'd have to beg him to participate."

Even as the sight warmed her heart, it didn't quite touch the sadness burrowed in her soul.

After chasing after the *youngies* for the better part of an hour, Abram needed a break. Hot and tired, he called for a time-out.

Hat in hand, he wiped his perspiring brow as he walked toward the rest area. The games were winding down, and people were drifting toward the picnic tables.

Glancing around, he caught sight of Maddie. Laughing and chatting with the other women, she had clearly settled into the group.

Struck by her grace, he couldn't help but stare. And no wonder. Maddie Baum was a beauty, with striking, wide blue eyes and a smattering of freckles across her pert nose. He also couldn't help but notice a couple of single fellows trying to catch her attention. Blushing, she shook her head, sending them on their way.

He frowned. It was natural other men would be attracted to her. The Amish believed large families were a blessing, and members of the community were encouraged to marry young.

A hand suddenly clapped him on the shoulder.

"Back in your thoughts again?" Rolf asked.

The interruption caused him to jump a little. "Sorry. Guess I was."

Chuckling, his older brother waved a hand. "Oh, I've figured out where your thoughts have been wandering." One corner of his mouth curved upward. "Can't miss that look on your face. You've got your eye on the new girl."

Brow knotting, a quick burst of air flared Abram's nostrils. "Am I that transparent?"

"Can't say that I blame you," Rolf continued. "And Lavinia says she comes from Pennsylvania Amish."

He let a shrug do his speaking. "Something like that."

Rolf nudged him. "You should go talk to her."

Abram shied back. "A pretty girl like her… She's not going to look twice at a fellow like me."

It was true. Maddie Baum was a rare beauty. And she had Amish roots, so it wouldn't exactly cause a scandal if he chose to court her.

Rolf gave another nudge. "You're not walking over there to propose. Just go and say hello."

Panic seized his confidence, freezing him in his tracks. All at once his stomach was full of knots, and his feet turned to stone blocks. "She's busy helping feed the *kinder*," he mumbled. "I don't want to bother her."

Rolf released a pent-up sigh of exasperation. "I'm reminded of a bit of Proverbs," he said, leaning in close. "'A merry heart doeth good like a medicine: but a broken spirit drieth the bones.' It isn't your face holding you back. It's your own self-pity. Unless you get over it and have confidence in yourself, you're going to be a lonely *der greis*."

A pause momentarily silenced their conversation as a rush of images unfurled through Abram's mind. His brother's words echoed in the depths of his psyche: *a lonely old man.* Suddenly, all his tomorrows stretched ahead of him, empty and dark.

"Stop beating yourself up and get on with your life."

"Do you think she'd give me a chance?"

"Why wouldn't she?" Rolf said, scratching a bare patch of skin beneath his lower lip. "*Gott* counsels us not to look at a man's outward appearance but at his heart. A true woman of the Lord won't even notice the scars on your face, but she will see your kind soul. You are a *gut* man. And when you find the right *fraulein*, you will know it."

"You think so?"

Rolf crinkled his nose. "I know so. Now, go. Just be yourself."

Walking on numb legs, Abram strode into the group. "*Hallo*," he greeted. "You look busy."

Staffing the coolers handing out drinks, Maddie retrieved a bottle of water. "You look thirsty."

Abram accepted the bottle. Cracking the cap, he took a long drink. "Think I've lost ten pounds running after the *kinder*."

"You're so patient with them. I've never seen Josh play like that before. You really got him into the game."

He glanced around, catching sight of Josh mixing with the other kids. The shy child who'd arrived had changed dramatically, now chatting a mile a minute with the other boys.

"I think it helps having *kind* his own age. If he sees others doing it, then he knows he can, too."

"I agree. I think he's glued himself to Hiram and Hershel."

Abram laughed. The boys belonged to his *bruder* Samuel and were a rambunctious pair. "*Ach*, the twins. Between the two of them, they are full of mischief. And they are so alike, you can't tell one from the other."

Remembrance glinted in the depths of Maddie's gaze. "That's what my *opa* used to say about me and my sister."

Surprise lifted his brows. "You're a twin?"

"*Ja*. I had a sister. Margaret."

"Had?"

"She passed, years ago. It was, um, sudden." Expression tensing, she fell to silence.

Embarrassed to be prying, Abram brushed aside his bangs, which were damp with perspiration. His skin felt tight. Suffocating. He hadn't meant to bring back bad memories.

"I'm sorry," he spluttered, unsure what to say. "I didn't mean to upset you."

"You didn't upset me. Seeing Hershel and Hiram playing just bought back a lot of memories of my own childhood. Happy ones. That's why I moved back to an Amish community. I want Josh to have good memories to look back on when he is grown."

Abram didn't have a chance to reply—infant pressed against her shoulder, Lavinia interrupted. "You two had better grab some food before it's gone."

"Well, I guess we need to eat." Abram patted his stomach. "I'm starving." He glanced to Maddie. "How about you?"

The corners of her eyes crinkled in the most appealing way. "Same."

They strolled to the picnic tables, joining the rest of the folks. Everyone stood, waiting their turn to serve themselves.

Picking up a couple of paper plates and plastic cutlery, Abram offered her one.

She accepted. "Everything looks so good. I don't know that I'll be able to pick from so much."

"Then have a little bit of everything." There was so much food, it was hard to choose his favorite. Of course, each woman had tried to outdo the others, presenting her best dishes.

Maddie went for the shepherd's pie with a side of macaroni and cheese. "It's been so long since I've had a good *hirtenkuchen*. I've tried to make it, but I could never match my *maummi*'s recipe."

Filling his plate, Abram led the way to an empty bench. When Maddie took a seat beside him, his pulse bumped up a notch. Here he was, sitting with the prettiest girl in the park. Amazing.

Flustered, he folded his hands over the plate balanced on his lap. *"Bless this meal and all the new friends we have made today, Lord."*

Before taking a single bite, Maddie, too, lowered her head. "Amen."

They ate in comfortable silence.

Sneaking a glance when he could, Abram couldn't help but be impressed. Quiet and well-spoken, Maddie fit right into the group. It made him wonder—why had she left her own community?

Curiosity niggled. A million questions crowded into his mind. He wanted to know so much more about her but dared not ask.

The evening drizzled away as the sun dipped farther below the horizon. As the event began to wind down, everyone helped clean up, discarding the trash and packing up the leftovers. Families dispersed, heading toward home. By now the park was almost completely abandoned. The clingy summer heat had dissipated, replaced by the cool velvet cloak of twilight.

Reluctant to see the evening end, Abram lingered. The last few precious minutes with Maddie were winnowing away, and he wanted to soak up every second.

Loaded down with extra food, Maddie walked toward her car. Waving to his new friends, Josh skipped ahead. One of the older boys had given him a hand-carved horse, explaining that he'd made it with nothing more than a piece of wood and a whittling blade.

Stacking the dishes so they wouldn't tip over, Maddie buckled Josh into his booster seat.

"Thank you for inviting us," she said as she walked around to the driver's side. "I really enjoyed it.

Unwilling to say goodbye, Abram shoved his hands in his pockets and shuffled his feet. "I'm glad you both came."

Maddie grinned. "Me, too." Sliding behind the wheel, she rolled down the window and waved. "Thank you again."

Shoving her key in the ignition, she twisted it and tapped the accelerator. The most the tired engine managed was a weak *erg-erg-erg* sound. The headlights flickered and then dimmed. Then they went out completely.

The old vehicle was going nowhere.

Unable to ignore her distress, Abram cocked his head. "That doesn't sound good."

Stepping back out, she released a long sigh of frustration. "I can't believe this is happening. It was running fine earlier."

He tapped on hood. "Why don't I take a look?"

"You know about cars?"

A chuckle rolled past his lips. "The Amish are a lot more high-tech nowadays. I'm no mechanic, but I can fix a few things."

"Would you mind?"

"Sure. Got a flashlight?"

"I do." Digging into the glove compartment, she pulled one out and flicked it on.

"Open it up."

She did as instructed. "I hope it's nothing bad."

"We'll see." He shined the torch onto the engine. A mess greeted his gaze. The connections were crusty, and stray wires stuck out every which way. It was a wonder the vehicle was still on the road. The poor old thing looked like it was held together with baling wire and duct tape.

"What do you think it is?" she asked, peering into the depth.

"Could be as simple as the battery cables being corroded, or a bad fuse. Or it could be the alternator. I would imagine it needs a thorough tune-up to make sure it's safe."

Blowing out a breath, she angled one hip against the car. Desolation haunted her expression. "I sure didn't need this right now." As she clasped her hands, her slender fingers twisted with unspoken worry.

"Of course not." He lowered the hood back into place. "Why don't you let me give you a ride? There's no church tomorrow, so the entire day is free. I'll ask my *bruder* Elam to work on it. He's a mechanic and should be able to handle it."

Shaking her head, Maddie nibbled her lower lip. "That's a generous offer, but I can't afford to pay to have it fixed now." She straightened to her full height, which barely reached to his shoulder. "I have legs, and they work just fine."

Unwilling to leave her stranded, he pressed on. "I have nothing to do tomorrow. And neither does Elam. I'm sure he can get you back on the road."

Hesitating, she angled her chin, showing the stubbornness of a barnyard mule. "I don't take advantage of people."

"It's not taking advantage if someone is offering the help," he countered, hoping to set her mind at ease. A woman alone in a strange town with a small child and a broken-down car—the situation must be frightening beyond belief for her.

Maddie glanced over to her car and then back to him. Her resolve faltered. "I've got a kid and a vehicle that doesn't run, and I'm just plain beat." She threw her hands up in sheer frustration. "I don't have a single person I can call for help."

"You could just say yes."

Maddie hesitated.

Her *youngie* did not.

Little pitchers apparently had big ears.

Clapping, Josh popped through the window. Somehow, he'd worked his way out of his booster seat and was determined to take part in the conversation. "Yes, please!"

Smiling past her frustration, Maddie graciously gave in. "Okay. You've talked me into it. I appreciate the offer." Pride shattering, relief lightened her worry.

"Then it's settled."

Abram returned her flashlight. For the first time in a long time, he didn't think twice about his face. Maddie had neither asked about his scars nor even acknowledged their presence. That alone gave him hope. Like a seed awakening after a long winter's slumber, he felt a sense of renewal deep in his spirit. Was it possible *Gott* was guiding him in a new direction?

He didn't yet have that answer.

But he wanted to find out.

Chapter Four

Maddie was a nervous wreck. She watched anxiously as Elam Mueller popped the hood and bent over her engine.

"Oh, my..." he said, fiddling with a few loose wires.

Noticing Elam's frustration, her stomach knotted. All she knew about cars was how to change a tire, check the oil and add water to the radiator. Past those three basics, she was clueless about mechanical things.

"I hope it's not bad."

Josh joined in, peering curiously. "Can you fix my mom's car?"

"Maybe. Maybe not." Elam walked over to his truck to retrieve his toolbox. "I'm not going to say anything until I've had a chance to look things over. Give me about half an hour, and I'll be able to tell you more."

When Abram and his brother had showed up, she was surprised to see them riding in a modern, gas-powered vehicle. However, it wasn't unusual for Amish to travel in cars. Although not allowed to drive themselves, many often hired drivers with trucks to help them move equipment a horse and wagon could not handle, or for longer trips where a buggy wouldn't be practical or welcome in traffic. Elam's huge dual-cab truck had easily towed her smaller vehicle to his garage on the Mueller property located about a mile outside Humble. Dressed in jeans, a T-shirt, a baseball cap and tennis shoes, Elam Mueller had clearly embraced *Englisch* ways.

Standing nearby, Abram gave her a reassuring nod. "Elam knows how to work on about everything with an engine. If anyone can get it running, he can."

Maddie pressed her hands together. "I'm praying hard he does."

"It's probably going to take a while for Elam to look it over." Abram pointed to a bench shaded by trees. "Why don't we get out of this sun?"

Wiping damp bangs off her forehead, she nodded. "I could use a break from the heat." At an hour past noon, the day was turning into a scorcher.

Following Abram to the bench, she looked around the Mueller property. Neat houses dotted the property, which was blanketed with lush grass and patches of wild brambles. Each home had its own individual look. Vegetable gardens were in abundance, as were the stalls and barns housing the horses and other livestock. The houses were spaced far enough apart so each family had their own space yet were close enough that a short walk was all it took to visit with neighbors. In the distance, a stream following a gentle downhill slope wound through the trees, filling a pond with icy water.

Struck by the calm and serene beauty of the wooded landscape, she smiled. "How long has your family lived here?"

"Gran'pa bought the land when he was a young man and raised his *kinder* here. Any time he got a little money, he purchased a few more acres to add to it. Whenever a Mueller comes of age, they get a piece to build on." He pointed to the houses, naming off the family members they belonged to.

"That's a lovely tradition."

"That's where I live." He pointed to a two-story home in the distance. White with small windows, it boasted a fenced-in deck facing the east. A quaint outhouse sat nearby.

"Is that what I think it is?"

He chuckled. "Yes, it is."

"Haven't used one of those since I was a kid."

"Gran'pa didn't want to move to a *dawdy haus* after *Maummi* passed. I moved in to help keep an eye on him. He doesn't like modern things, so the facilities are out-of-date. He's near eighty now, so it's easier to let him have his way."

"My grandparents were the same. My sister and I made many a trip to the outside loo in the middle of the night with a flashlight. I remember how scared we were some animal would attack us. And I learned to cook on a wood-burning stove."

Admiration lit his gaze. "I'm impressed."

"Sometimes I miss cooking that way. The food tasted so much better then."

"I agree. Except in summer, when it's so hot."

Maddie was about to reply when a burst of shouts and laughter cut through the air. She turned in time to see some of Abram's nieces and nephews skipping toward the garage. Each carried a homemade fishing pole and a small pail of bait. Lavinia and Samuel trailed in their wake, herding the crew.

"*Hallo*," Samuel greeted with a wave. "I see you and Elam got Maddie's car."

Abram waved back. "We did."

Infant on her hip, Lavinia ambled up. "Abram,

for shame! Why didn't you tell us Maddie and Josh were here? I'd have been out sooner to visit."

"I'm fine, really."

Lavinia shifted Sophie, popping a pacifier into the fussy infant's mouth. "Have you had lunch? I'll be glad to fix you and Josh something if you're hungry."

"We're fine, thank you."

"Well, if you're going to be outside, you'll need something to drink. How does a cold glass of sweet tea sound?"

"I could take some." Abram removed his hat and wiped his brow.

"Two glasses of iced tea coming up."

"Maybe you could throw in a handful of gingersnap cookies," he added hopefully.

"Of course." Lavinia turned to her older brother. "Sam, watch the *kinder* while I'm gone."

"I've got this."

Losing interest in the car, Josh rushed to examine the strange new things the other children carried. "What have you got?"

Hiram held out a fishing pole carved from a tree branch. A piece of string and a hook dangled from the end. The other children, including Zeke and little Eli, each had a pole.

"Goin' fishing."

Hershel held up his pail. "I've got worms!"

Peeking in the pail, Josh scrunched up his face. "Worms?"

"Yeah, you put 'em on the hook, and the fish eat 'em," little Eli exclaimed.

Excited by the idea, Josh looked up at Maddie with an eager face. "Can I go fish, too?"

When she glanced toward the pond, hesitation shadowed Maddie's face.

"It's safe enough," Abram said. "The pond isn't deep. The *youngies* can sit on the dock and cast their lines."

To help seal the deal, Samuel held out the pole he carried. "Josh can use mine. It's a little long, but I think he's big enough to handle it."

Maddie gave a nod of assent. "You can. But be careful and don't go in the water."

Samuel handed Josh his pole. "Here you go. All yours."

The children raced off, chattering and laughing.

"Don't worry. I've got this." Winking, Samuel added, "Looking forward to a mess of fish, homemade fries and slaw later tonight."

"Sounds good." Abram turned to Maddie. "Maybe you and Josh would like to stay for supper. Nothing better than a catfish fry."

She shook her head. "I'd hate to impose on your family any more than we already have."

"No imposition at all," Samuel said.

Carrying a tray loaded with a pitcher and glasses, Lavinia caught the tail end of the conversation. Rolf's oldest daughter, Trisha, trailed behind her with a plate of cookies.

"Couple more feet under the table are always welcome." Lavinia set the tray on a nearby picnic-style table. Tipping the pitcher, she poured fresh-brewed tea into tall glasses filled with ice.

"I guess we'd better get to fishing if we're going to feed this crew." Whistling a tune, Samuel walked toward the pond. Already the children had baited and cast their lines.

A curse that caught everyone's attention followed the clank of metal against metal.

Wrench in hand, Elam frowned fiercely. "What a stubborn thing!"

Abram's brow wrinkled with annoyance. "Elam! There are ladies here. Watch your language."

His youngest brother flashed a guilty grin. "Excuse me. I was just fighting with a few rusted bolts."

"I hope the car won't be too much trouble," Maddie said.

Snorting a laugh, Elam brushed off her worry. "It's just bein' a little ornery."

Lavinia delivered the tea. "Drink up. And don't forget the gingersnaps, Trisha."

"Sorry." The shy teen held out the plate, offering around the home-baked cookies.

"This will hit the spot." Abram drank down a gulp of tea. "What do you think?"

"I can see why your family settled here," Maddie said, nibbling the edge of a cookie. "I'm glad Josh is getting a chance to do all the things we couldn't do in the city. I want him to appreciate nature."

"Bring him over to play anytime," Lavinia invited. "There's a lot for the kids to do, so we'll keep him busy. And I've always got a pot of coffee on for visiting."

"Oh, I'd hate to be a bother."

Lavinia waggled a scolding finger. "It's rude to say no when someone's inviting you."

"Everyone has been so kind to me and Josh. We've been on our own so long, I guess I've forgotten what it's like to socialize."

A shout drew Lavinia's attention.

"Lavinia, I need you! Sophie's fussing." Standing on the porch with his infant daughter, Josiah Simmons anxiously sought out his wife.

"*Ach*, that man. Ask him to watch his own *kind* for a few minutes and he falls apart." Shaking her head, she hurried away to placate her spouse.

"Nervous *dat*?" Maddie asked, watching Lavinia take control of her squirming child.

"I'm afraid Josiah hasn't got the knack for taking care of *kinder*," Abram said. "Ask him to change a nappy and he almost faints with horror."

"It's work to get them raised. But it's such a joy as they begin to grow and discover new things."

As if to second her words, the shouts and laughter of the *youngies* carried across the distance.

Cocking his head, Abram smiled at the sounds of laughter echoing up for the pond. "I think the *kinder* are having a fine time. I bet they're catching a lot of fish."

"Hope so." Maddie rose, brushing stray crumbs off her skirt. Seeing her car in pieces, she winced over the engine parts Elam had scattered on the ground. "So, your brother likes mechanical things?"

"Elam fell in love with engines when he was little. Carl Williams lets him work a couple of days a week at his shop as an apprentice. He's wanting to open his own place someday."

"And your family's okay with that?"

"Of course. Bishop Graber encourages members of the community to take a close look at both sides before making the decision to be baptized. Just because he doesn't want to be Amish doesn't make Elam an outcast. He will always be a member of the *familie*. The Bible says the heart of man plans his way, but the Lord establishes his steps. Elam's on a fine path. He's chosen a solid profession and can support himself and his future wife. Save for Gran'pa kicking a fit, no one's ashamed of his choice."

Throat visibly tightening with emotion, Maddie blinked hard. "My community was so strict and unbending. Anyone who chooses to go *Englisch* is kept at arm's length."

Elam strode up. "I've got some answers about your vehicle," he announced, wiping his hands on a shop towel.

Maddie tensed. "I hope it's good news."

He tucked the greasy rag in his back pocket. "Well, I guess you could say it's half and half."

"Meaning?"

"Meaning the car is fixable, but it's going to take some work. Best I can tell, it needs a new alternator, new belts, a battery and some wiring. Could also use an oil and filter change and a set of tires, too."

Dismay crept through her. "I had no idea it was so bad. I know it's an old car, but I was hoping to get a few more years out of it."

"Oh, I can get it running."

"You can?"

"Yeah. No problem. I think I can get some

parts out of the salvage yard. The rest I will have to get at the auto shop."

"How long will that take?"

"Don't know." Elam stuck his hands in his pockets and rocked back on his heels. "I've got a couple of buddies who can help, so it shouldn't take long."

Maddie accepted his assessment. With her car out of commission, it would be difficult to find a job. Although Humble was not nearly as large as the city they'd left behind, it also didn't have the conveniences of a larger metropolitan area. There were no trains, subways or buses to catch. Without a vehicle, her search for work would be limited by how far she could reasonably walk to reach her destination. Traveling on foot might not harm her, but the weather would—Wisconsin was all about blazing summers and cold, snowy winters.

"Well, it is what it is. It's a blessing you even know what to do. But that throws a monkey wrench in my plans. I'd hoped to start looking for a job Monday morning."

"Do you mind if I ask what you do?" Abram asked.

"I was an assistant manager of a dry-cleaning establishment. I was hoping to find something like that."

"You have experience with customer service?"

She laughed. "More than I care to admit."

"Maybe I could help. I had a couple of employees at the market quit recently and haven't had a chance to fill the positions yet. I need someone with computer and customer service experience who can handle the phones and invoicing of orders that come in for delivery. Would you be interested?"

"Are you offering me a job?"

"*Ja.* I am."

Maddie didn't hesitate. The little bit of money she had wouldn't last much longer. The sooner she got to work, the sooner she could get back on a steady financial footing. Didn't matter what the wages or hours were. Knowing the Amish, she was sure he'd be a fair employer.

"I accept. When do I start?"

Abram laughed. "We're closed on Sundays and Mondays, so how's Tuesday morning sound?"

She grinned. "I'm in."

They had barely finished shaking on the deal when the *youngies* rushed back from the lake, eager to show off their bounty.

Though he hadn't caught the biggest, Josh was excited about the wriggling catfish he'd pulled in. His grin was a mile wide.

The rest of the day passed in a blur of fellowship and family fun. The evening meal was delicious. Everyone ate until there wasn't a single bite left. Icy glasses of lemonade and tea washed everything down. Gran'pa Amos was in a fair mood, too, telling tales about the monster catfish in the pond that had taken him thirty years to hook.

By the time Abram and his brother drove her and Josh home, Maddie was relieved she'd made another step toward making a home in Humble.

"I can't believe I'm working here," Maddie said, pinning on her name tag. "Thank you for giving me a chance and arranging for the employee carpool to pick me up. That's one less thing to worry about right now."

Riding along with her new coworkers, she'd learned that Mueller's Amish Market had served the community for over sixty years, expanding from an outdoor vendors' stall into a large warehouse-type building. Save for common dry goods such as sugar, flour and baking powder, most every item was homegrown or made by hand.

"I'm happy you agreed. When Cassie quit, she really left me in a lurch." Abram motioned with a hand. "Your office is right this way."

"I have an office?" Maddie asked, trailing him down a busy hall. Behind the scenes, the market was a hive of activity as employees prepared for the day ahead. A couple of clerks hurried by pushing dollies loaded with a variety of produce.

"You do." Leading the way, he pointed toward a desk with a computer, large monitor, printer and multiline phone. Pens, pads of paper, a calculator and other office supplies were within easy reach.

"I wasn't expecting an Amish business to be so high-tech."

"Well, we understand our *Englisch* workers want the convenience of electronics that make their jobs easier. You and Charles—he's our accountant—could do your jobs with just a pen, paper and calculators, I suppose. But it would be slow and inefficient."

"True."

"In the market front, it's different. We strive to give our customers an authentic Amish experience. That's why we use old-fashioned cash registers and other nonelectrical devices. We also do our deliveries with a horse and buggy. Also, no Amish employee is expected to work with any devices they feel uncomfortable using."

He leaned over the desk, explaining the details of her job. Taking orders over the phone and by email, she'd handle the billing and payment processing for the items going out.

"I think I can do that."

"This is new for us, so we're still hitting some snags. But the market really has a chance to grow if we do this right."

"I think it's a wonderful way to reach customers."

"I believe so." Shaking his head, Abram blew out a sigh. "Gran'pa is fighting the idea every step of the way. He thinks people should come to us and not the other way around. He also doesn't care to hire *Englischers* and does his best to make them miserable until they get fed up and quit."

"Your grandfather can be ornery."

"Close your office door and he won't bother you. He may not agree, but I am hoping to expand into selling our goods online. For now, we only service the local area, but I hope this idea can grow as we work out the logistics."

"Sounds like a challenge."

"I'm praying I've found the right person to help make it happen."

"I'll do my best."

After getting Maddie settled in, Abram went to take care of other tasks. There was no reason to hang over her shoulder. If she had a question, he'd be available to help.

Grabbing a stack of orders, he handed them out to his runners, instructing them to get the items shopped and ready for loading. Although they'd only been offering the service a short time, it was taking off. People who had busy schedules, the elderly and those who didn't want to shop for themselves had taken notice after he'd placed ads in the local newspaper. After the website went up, they'd begun receiving inquiries from folks out of state, too. People wanted authentic Amish food and other goods. Why not find a way to get them into their hands?

Between answering administrative inquiries and dealing with customers, he was pulled in a dozen different directions. Hours disappeared in the blink of an eye. By the time noon rolled around, he was ready to sit down a few minutes.

Heading to the break room, Abram stopped to check on Maddie. She was on the phone, speaking with a customer. She easily handled the conversation, speaking in *Deitsch*. She spoke clearly and politely, efficiently taking a customer's order even as she gently inquired about items they might have forgotten.

Admiration filled him. *She definitely knew how to upsell.*

Ending the call, she slipped off the headset and put it aside.

"How's it going?"

"Good." She finished jotting the last of her notes. "Busy. The phone hasn't stopped ringing all morning."

"You'll get a little break from that since the cutoff is noon," Abram said. "After lunch, I'll head out and deliver the orders."

"I have to admit, I could use a breather."

"If you would like, we could grab a bite at the café across the street."

"Actually, I brought my own." Maddie pushed away from the desk. "I thought I'd eat in that rest area by the bank. I could use a little sun and some fresh air."

Disappointment washed over him. "Of course. Enjoy your meal."

"Why don't you join me? Mrs. Graff packed me two giant liverwurst sandwiches. I already know it's too much for me to eat by myself."

He perked up. "I can throw in the drinks and dessert."

"Give me ten minutes to freshen up, and I'll meet you outside."

"Deal."

The market was stocked with the best meats, cheeses, desserts and other produce and products sought out by *Englisch* shoppers. The business had grown exponentially through the years. People who came to visit the thriving Amish town often ended up coming back to live in Humble.

Stopping at the counter, he asked Gretl to wrap up a few fried pies. Stuffed with a fruit filling, the crust was folded over and fried before being dipped in a sweet glaze. Blueberry and cherry were especially tasty.

Snagging a few bottles of water, he headed to pay for his food. As they were shorthanded again, Gran'pa Amos was working one of the registers.

"Just dessert for your meal?" The old man slid the purchase into a small paper bag.

"I'm having lunch with Maddie. She's got the sandwiches, and I promised to bring the rest."

Accepting a ten-dollar bill, Amos punched a few buttons on the cash register. "How is she handling her first day?"

"I have no complaints. I think our customers will be pleased we have an *Englischer* who speaks *Deitsch*, too."

Amos carefully counted out his change. "I'm glad it's working out."

"I have a *gut* feeling about her."

"Talk is she's from Pennsylvania Amish folks. Has she said why she left?"

"I don't know, and it isn't my business to ask. Why?"

"I know how you are. You jump in without

question to lend a helping hand. The Lord cautions us to have care against those whose motives might not be pure. Don't let your desire to do good blind you into being led astray."

"I don't think helping someone in need is leading me astray."

Amos sucked at his dentures. "Just make sure you know what she's about. We don't need any trouble."

Another customer moved into line, prompting an end to the conversation.

Collecting his purchase, Abram walked through the market. A slew of pesky thoughts buzzed through his mind. The old man had certainly put a bee under his bonnet.

Maddie had come from an Amish community nobody knew much about. The few details she'd given left many questions unanswered. The most telling thing she'd said was that there was nothing left for her and Josh in Pennsylvania.

Then, the offhanded remark hadn't meant much.

Now, it might have a deeper implication than he'd initially realized.

The only reason he could think of that would cause a person to abandon their kin would be because all *familie* ties had been cut. And that only happened when someone broke the rules of the *Ordnung* and was put under the *bann*.

Fine hairs rising on the back of his neck, his insides withered.

Was it possible Maddie Baum had been shunned?

Chapter Five

By the end of her first day, Maddie was exhausted. Mueller's Amish Market was a busy place and keeping up with her duties was a challenge. Although she'd worried the computer might present a problem, she found the invoicing and ordering software easy to navigate. The biggest challenge was making sure she entered all figures correctly. Between processing orders and checking the merchandise to be delivered, there was always something to do. The brisk pace made the day go faster.

All in all, she felt she'd done well. Occasionally, she hit a snag. When that happened, Abram or the accountant, Charles Blair, patiently walked her through the issue.

Come five o'clock, she was ready to call it quits. Once she made it home, her goal was to spend a few hours with Josh and, hopefully, crawl into bed early.

Walking to the break room to punch out, she chatted with her coworkers. Though it had taken a few hours to break the ice, they had warmed to her once they'd discovered she could converse with them in their own language. Only Gran'pa Amos had avoided her.

Heading toward the rear exit, Maddie joined the flow of employees. To get back to Mrs. Graff's boardinghouse, she'd have to take one of the vans Abram hired to shuttle people to and from work. Parking a dozen or more horses and buggies all day often wasn't feasible. The solution was to hire *Englisch* drivers to get everyone where they needed to be. As the town grew and traffic increased, more and more Amish were turning to more practical solutions for transportation. Bicycles were frequently used, as were e-scooters, among others. If nothing else, the Amish were clever in solving their issues without violating the *Ordnung*.

Standing in line, she waited her turn to climb onboard. There was a general chat going on among employees who wanted the driver to stop at a popular fast-food restaurant so they could grab something.

Thinking burgers and fries sounded pretty

good, Maddie was surprised when Abram stepped into the line.

She stiffened. The only real snag in her day was lunch, and she hadn't quite figured out why. When Abram had agreed to join her, she had envisioned a pleasant chat over the meal. But by the time he'd joined her, his mood had shifted. Sitting as far away from her as he could on their shared bench, he'd wolfed down his food in silence. He barely looked at her, and when he spoke, he was civil but distant. After an excruciating half hour, he'd excused himself, mumbling something about the deliveries. Tipping his hat, he'd thanked her for the sandwich and departed.

What had she done wrong? Had she accidentally caused some offense?

Whatever it was, she was determined to get some clarification.

Even if it meant he might fire her.

Everyone boarded, taking a seat. As Maddie buckled herself in, she noticed Abram had taken the seat directly opposite hers. One of the clerks sat in the middle, separating them.

Ready to go, the *Englisch* driver pulled out of the parking lot and into traffic.

Settling in for the ride, Maddie stared out the window. The driver made his rounds through town.

As the young man sitting between them exited

at his stop, she glanced across the empty seat. She and Abram were the last ones on the shuttle.

"Excuse me, miss," the driver said. "Could I get your address again?"

"Bethel Lane. Mrs. Graff's boardinghouse." Most of the older neighborhoods had streets with biblical names, a tradition begun when Humble was still mostly an Amish settlement.

The driver punched the address into his GPS. "That's across town. Be about a twenty-minute drive."

"Thanks."

The ride continued.

Maddie glanced at Abram. Glasses slipped down to the end of his nose, he read from a pocket-size Bible.

"Good devotional today?"

"I was led back to the epistle to the Romans," he said. "'Let us not therefore judge one another any more.'"

She offered a smile. "A *gut* lesson for all of us," she said, falling easily into the *Deitsch*.

Sighing, Abram lowered the book. "Maddie, I hope you will understand, but there's something I have to ask you."

Puzzled, she nodded. "I'll be glad to answer any questions you have."

Using a single finger, he pushed his glasses back into place before looking her straight in the eyes. "Earlier today, I was speaking with Gran'pa, and he mentioned we don't know much about you or Josh. Something you said earlier came to mind, and it set me to thinking."

"About what?"

"Please understand I am not condemning you. But coming from the Amish, you know there are some things we just can't just ignore about a person. Especially one of our own."

The sinking feeling in the pit of her stomach intensified.

"Of course. I understand the Amish way of life and how behavior is disciplined."

"Then you'll understand why I have to ask you a very important question." Pausing, Abram cleared his throat. Finally, he said, "Did you leave your community because you were shunned?"

Shunned.

The word struck like a slap.

A chill wormed its way toward her core even as numbness took control of her limbs. Settling inside her chest, it clenched her heart. She shivered and instinctively rubbed her hands over her arms to still the rising goose bumps on her skin.

Oh, no.

Once again, her past had reared its ugly head.

She had never lied to Abram or tried to mislead him. But she had deliberately skipped over parts of her life.

Thinking back, she understood why he'd been so distant and uncomfortable during lunch. In the Amish community, to be shunned meant that members of the community could not socialize or do any business with a person who'd been excommunicated.

"I'm sorry. But I have to know."

"I've not been shunned," she answered in a quiet tone, careful that her reply wouldn't reach the ears of the *Englisch* driver. "But my *mamm* was."

"I see." Sympathy lined Abram's face. "Would you mind telling me why?"

Shame filled her. She'd always felt her *mamm*'s turbulent life and choices had led to her own sister repeating many of the same mistakes. She worried her lower lip, trying to get the words together.

"My *mamm*, Emmaline Baum, fell in love with an *Englisch* man when she was seventeen. Unfortunately, the affair was a short one, and they broke up. After that, she found out she was pregnant. A short time later, she gave birth to me and my sister, Margaret."

Abram remained silent, giving her a nod to indicate he would listen without interruption.

"After we were born, the bishop paired her with an older widower who agreed to take her as his *frau* and raise her *kinder* as his own. My mother was baptized before the marriage, as was expected. But the day before she was to be wed, she ran away." Unbidden tears suddenly blurred her vision. She blinked hard to clear them away. "She left no note. But she did leave me and my sister behind."

Abram raised a hand. "You need not say more. I can see it is painful for you."

Maddie swiped at her eyes. "No, I want to tell you the rest," she said. "I want to tell you how Margaret and I were raised by our dear *opa* and *maummi*. For years, they loved us as their own and did their best to raise us. But when we were twelve, my *mamm* came back. She had an *Englisch ehmann* and wanted us to live with them in California. She threatened my grandparents with the law, saying she would sue for custody. They let us go to keep the peace. Because she was shunned, *Mamm* told us we were, too. She said we could never see our grandparents again."

"I'm so sorry." Reaching into a pocket, Abram pulled out a handkerchief. "Please."

She gratefully accepted, dabbing at her eyes. The pain and shame of her past had always felt like a millstone around her neck. "*Danke.* I apologize for burdening you with that."

"Not a burden at all. I am glad to know your story, because it gives me a chance to clear up the misinformation your *mamm* gave you."

She lowered the handkerchief. "Misinformation? I—I don't understand."

"You've been misled into believing the shunned couldn't be forgiven their trespasses. That isn't true. Even those under the *bann* have their place among us. In time, they may even be forgiven and welcomed back into the community once they have done their penance."

"Then *Gott* would forgive me for leaving the church?"

"I doubt He would judge an innocent child so unfairly. And everyone deserves a second chance. The Bible says if we confess our sins, the Lord will cleanse us of all unrighteousness."

His words, so badly needed, lightened the burden of shame she'd carried for years.

The pressure that had been building in her psyche suddenly burst.

A tear escaped her control, then another. Shaking overwhelmed her fragile composure. Dropping her gaze, she wept. Abram didn't know it, but it relieved her to know she had not committed an unforgivable sin against her *familie* and community.

Aside from her sister, few people knew the entire story. Her grandparents had passed years ago. Her *mamm*, too, had disappeared, staying barely a year with them in California before packing and leaving in the middle of the night.

Emmaline Baum hated being married to one man and never liked staying in one place for too long.

Their befuddled stepfather had done his best to finish raising them, helping them adapt to their new way of living. He'd hired a tutor to help them study for their GEDs. Thanks to him, they'd also learned how to drive, how to open a bank account and handle money. A few years later, he'd succumbed to lung cancer. He left a small insurance policy, one that kindly named her and Margaret beneficiaries. With no other relatives to turn to, it was all they had to get them started in life.

Putting her share into savings, Maddie had gotten a job at a day care. She loved *kinder*, and caring for them gave her immense pride. She also dreamed of saving enough money to go to community college and get a real degree.

Margaret, on the other hand, seemed to have a lot of her mother in her. She'd immediately spent her money on clothes and cosmetics. Young and flirty, Margaret embraced the vices the *Englisch* world had to offer.

Then she met Cash Harper, the man she would call the love of her life.

The boyfriend who would also end her life.

Much to Abram's relief, Maddie Baum wasn't one of the shunned. Nor did he believe she'd be deceptive enough to lie about the matter. The bishop of her church would have a record of all excommunications, which would be easy enough for Bishop Graber to make an inquiry about.

From the sound of things, she and her sister had gotten a rough deal. He couldn't imagine how hard it would be for the two girls to be torn away from the only life they'd ever known and then thrust into a whole new world. If ever there was a person so in need of a kind word, he believed she qualified.

"I did not mean to cause you pain. Please accept my apology for doubting you."

She wiped red-rimmed eyes. "I understand why you would have such suspicions, and you were right to question me. I know associating with a shunned person would jeopardize your own standing in the church. I would never want to do anything that would get you in trouble."

"If you would like, I can arrange for you to speak with Bishop Graber. Perhaps it would help ease your mind. He would be happy to counsel you, I know."

"I've been afraid to go to church because I worried someone would find out about my *mamm*'s shunning."

"No one should ever be afraid to seek out the truth."

"I thought I had committed a sin *Gott* couldn't

forgive." She offered a hesitant smile. "Maybe there's hope for me after all."

"I believe *Gott* strengthens us through difficult times. Though we may not understand it at the time, there is a reason for what happens in our lives."

Maddie drew a steadying breath. "*Danke* for your kindness." She reached out and laid a hand on his arm. "I didn't mean to disappoint you."

Her touch, so unexpected, sent a pulse of warmth through Abram's veins, bumping up his heartbeat a notch. The air in his lungs grew thin. It seemed he'd forgotten how to breathe. All he could focus on were her eyes and the pain lingering in the depths of her gaze.

Embarrassed by his reaction, he forced his gaze away. When he'd been baptized, he had committed himself to following the Lord. It was a lifelong promise, one he intended to keep until the day he passed from this earth. The gospels promised that *Gott* had a plan for every soul He created. The Lord had a path for him to follow. Keeping his feet going forward and his faith focused would lead him to the life he was meant to live.

Letting his heart lead his head would be foolish.

The van hit a bump, jarring him back to the present.

"Next stop," the driver announced before pulling the vehicle up to the curb.

He tucked his Bible back in his pocket. "Looks like we're here."

Maddie gathered her purse. "I appreciate the ride home."

"Most everyone does." He slid the curbside door open. "Myself included," he continued, stepping out to allow her to exit. "After being in a horse and buggy all day for deliveries, it gives me a chance to read my Bible and reflect on the evening's study."

"I think I might try that myself." Slipping past the empty seats, she stepped onto the pavement.

He hesitated, not quite ready to send her off on her own. "May I walk you to the door?"

She gave him a watery smile. "I think that would be all right." She pointed to the cobbled path leading around to the back of the rambling house. "I've rented Mrs. Graff's attic loft. The entrance is through a side door leading to the kitchen."

"My cousins did the renovations. I heard them say it was quite a job to turn that old, dusty attic into a living space."

"They did a great job. I was lucky to find it. I'm thankful the rent is reasonable."

"Wanetta has a reputation for being fair with her boarders. I've known plenty of girls who have lived here through the years, and they all praise her generous spirit."

Maddie paused at the foot of the steps. A cornucopia of tantalizing scents drifted through the kitchen window. "Smells like Mrs. Graff is getting supper ready. I'm sure she'll invite you to eat. Would you care to stay?"

"I would hate to intrude."

"No intrusion. And I'm sure Josh would love to see you. He's talked of nothing but that fish he caught." Breaking into a laugh, she spread her hands, showing a size. "In his mind, that catfish was bigger than a whale. I think it was the best day he's ever had."

Her words warmed him. From what he'd seen, Josh was a bright, active *boi*, eager to learn new things. "You and Josh are welcome to come and fish anytime you like."

"Your *familie* has been so open and generous to us. But really, I wouldn't want to wear out our welcome."

"If it makes your *youngie* happy, why not?"

"I am sure Josh would love to go fishing again." Her nose crinkled. "He wants to start digging up worms."

"Something it sounds like you're not quite into."

"Sometimes it's hard for me to get into *boi*

things. You know what they say *jungen* are made of—snips, snails and puppy dog tails."

Abram laughed. His own nephews were always into something, much to their mothers' lament. Samuel's wife, Frannie, always had her hands full with her precocious twins and often threatened to hang the boys up in the barn by the scruff of their necks to keep them out of mischief.

The screen door opened behind them. Wanetta stepped out onto the porch.

"*Ach*, I thought I heard voices."

"We didn't mean to startle you," Maddie apologized.

Wanetta wiped her damp hands on a dish towel. "*Guten abend*, Abram."

Abram tipped his hat. "*Guten abend.* I hope you don't mind, but I was just seeing Miss Baum to the door."

"*Gut* of you to get her home." Frowning, her gaze traveled to Maddie. "When you have a moment, I need to speak with you."

"You don't look happy. Has something happened?"

The landlady pursed her lips. "It would probably be best if we spoke in private."

Abram took a step back. "I should get going."

"Actually, I'd like it if you would stay." Maddie glanced between the two of them. "Whatever you've got to say should be for all ears to hear."

Wanetta pursed her lips. "I'm afraid you're not going to be pleased, but I'm going to have to ask you to find another sitter for Josh."

"Oh, no." Shaking, Maddie sucked in a breath. "What happened?"

"That *youngie* is out of control," Wanetta said, waggling a finger. "I didn't take my eyes off him for ten minutes before he sneaked out and got into my henhouse. Broke all the eggs, he did, throwing them around. When I chastised him, he yelled and stamped his feet, saying he hated me and didn't like it here."

Maddie's expression crumbled. "Oh, Mrs. Graff, I am so sorry. I specifically told Josh he needed to mind you before I left for work."

"I hate to say it, but your *boi* has a stubborn streak and won't listen."

"I will pay you for the eggs he broke," Maddie said, attempting to extend an olive branch to the angry woman. "And anything else he damaged."

"That's fine. But you will have to find someone else to take care of him. I'm too old to be dealing with an out-of-control *kind*."

"I understand. And please accept my apology. I expected Josh to act better than he did. Where is he? I'll go have a talk with him."

Wanetta pointed to the backyard. "He said he

was going to run away, but he's hiding in the doghouse with Sully. I've been keeping an eye, and he hasn't made a peep for hours."

Attempting to put on a brave face, Maddie drew back her shoulders. "Thank you, Mrs. Graff. I appreciate everything you've done," she said, barely in control of her wobbling voice. "I'll make other arrangements for Josh while I'm at work."

"Sounds fine." Her piece said, the older woman headed back into her kitchen. "Supper will be on the table soon." She paused to add, "You and your driver are welcome to have a bite, if you care, Abram."

He tipped his hat again. "*Danke*. I appreciate the invitation."

When her landlady was out of earshot, Maddie said, "I am sorry you had to hear that."

"Sounds like your *boi* has had quite a day."

Defeated, she sat down on the steps and buried her head in her hands. "My first day on a new job, and he does this. What am I doing wrong?"

Sensing she needed an ear to bend, Abram sat down beside her. The driver could wait a few more minutes. Compensated for his time, he probably wouldn't mind.

"Josh, he is hard to handle, *ja*?"

Maddie raised her head. Spent by her outburst of emotion, she wiped her eyes.

"No judgment," he murmured. "I want to help, if you'll let me."

A twitch drew her mouth down. "Josh is one of those kids that gets bored really easy. His school counselor said it was ADHD. He's hyperactive. He was in some special programs. But with school out for the summer, I haven't had time to see what I could get him enrolled in here in Humble. I'm hoping to find a place for special-needs children."

Abram scratched his chin. "Sounds to me like Josh needs to be busy from sunup to sundown."

A shrug of defeat rolled off her shoulders. "I'll figure out something."

Touched by the note of despair in her voice, he cocked his head. "Why don't you let me talk to him?"

Doubt crept into her expression. "I don't think there's a thing you could say that would make him straighten up. I've begged and pleaded and bribed until I'm blue in the face." Despair touched her expression. "I don't know what to do anymore."

"Believe it or not, I know a little *boi* who was exactly like Josh."

"Really?"

"I swear, it's true. He was stubborn as a mule, and because he wanted his own way, he got in all sorts of trouble."

She gave him a curious glance. "What happened to him?"

Abram set his palm against his scarred cheek. "*Gott* gave him a lesson he wouldn't forget."

Visually tracking his gesture, comprehension dawned in the depths of her eyes. "You?"

"*Ja*," he admitted. "I was that *boi*."

Chapter Six

Maddie's brow rose with surprise. "You?" she asked through a half laugh of disbelief. "You were a *das blag*?"

Letting his hand drop, Abram nodded. "Yeah. I was a real brat. If there was trouble, you could bet I was the one to find it or cause it."

"I wouldn't have believed that of you."

"Oh, it's true. When we have a minute, I'll sit down and tell you about some of the things I did." He glanced toward the backyard. "For now, we should probably get Josh out of that doghouse."

"My son certainly picked an appropriate place to hide," she said, clucking her tongue. "But he probably won't come out easily. He's a stubborn kid, and when he digs in his heels, you just can't reason with him. I've tried everything, from time-outs to taking away his electronics, and nothing works."

Prodded by a distant memory, Abram frowned. Back when he was a kid, his *daed* had ruled with an iron fist. Nathan Mueller felt sparing the rod spoiled the child. Abram had gotten punished many times for his acts of disobedience. And the only thing that had accomplished was to make him more defiant. Then, he didn't want to be Amish. He wanted to be more like his *Englisch* friends and not stuck baling hay all day or working in the gardens pulling weeds.

"I was the same way."

Frustrated, Maddie threw up her hands. "Maybe he'll listen to a man. He's never had a father figure to guide him."

"Josh's *daed* was never in his life?"

Hesitation invaded her expression. "He was—briefly—after Josh was born. Now, he's not." She bit her lower lip. "We weren't married or anything."

Abram scrubbed a hand across his mouth. Though she'd answered with candor, her eyes dodged his. "I'm not meaning to pry."

As if steeling herself in preparation for a physical blow, Maddie drew her shoulders back. "Josh doesn't know his *daed.* At all." Pausing to gather her nerve, she angled her chin. "Excuse me for saying it, but I would be happy it if it stayed that way."

Abram had to admire her straightforward answers. She could have lied, made up some excuse as to why she and Josh were on their own, but she hadn't. She'd told the truth and hadn't flinched against the fallout.

"It's not for me to question your choices."

"For what it's worth, I'm doing all I can to give him a decent life." Though she smiled, sadness lingered in the depths of her gaze. "Sometimes it just feels like it'll never be good enough."

Abram cocked his head. He understood what it felt like to be an angry, out-of-place *youngie*. "I think I know what to say to him."

"Be my guest."

Nodding, he walked back to the waiting van. No reason to make the driver sit and twiddle his thumbs. Leaning in the window, he instructed the man to let his *familie* know he would be home late. Asking him to return in an hour, he sent the vehicle on its way.

"I'm sorry. I know it's been a long day and you'd like to go home."

He waved a hand. "Lavinia can give Gran'pa his supper. I think I can stay out late one night now and again."

Maddie glanced toward Mrs. Graff's backyard. "I hope you can talk some sense into him."

"I'll do my best."

Walking around to the back of the house, Abram passed through a locked gate.

Surrounded by a high fence painted in a stark white shade, a neatly trimmed lawn lapped against the boundaries of lush gardens. Bracketed between house and gardens was a place for the *kind* to play, complete with a play set for climbing and swinging and a sandbox with a few toys scattered about. A barn, a chicken coop, and a few other small buildings for keeping animals dotted the periphery of the property. A doghouse sat beneath a copse of trees. The spacious retreat was wreathed in shadows as the sun began its descent toward the horizon.

In the older neighborhoods, the acreage was spread out, giving the owners more space. Gardens were grown and livestock such as horses, goats, pigs and chickens were tended, just as on any farm, albeit on a smaller scale. When the town began to adapt to *Englisch* ways, many Amish residents were grandfathered in. This meant a slight bending of city code that allowed people to live in dwellings without access to electric power and, sometimes, indoor plumbing. Carved out of densely wooded land, the suburbs of Humble offered a slice of country living within a stone's throw of city limits.

Shutting the gate, he looked toward Josh's hiding place. The dog's kennel had been designed to look like a miniature version of the main house, complete with a gabled roof, a deck and a door. For a child, it doubled as a cozy place to play. He wasn't sure what he'd say to Josh or how he'd even engage the child, but he had an idea that might entice the *boi* out.

Ambling toward the sandbox, he knelt and picked up one of the toy shovels. "I'm wondering if there's any night crawlers here," he said, just loud enough to be heard. Silence. Abram tried again. "Gonna need some for fishing this weekend."

This time, he got a response.

"What's a night crawler?" Josh asked from within the depths of his hiding place.

Without looking back, Abram kept digging. As a kid, gathering fishing worms was one of the many simple pleasures he'd enjoyed growing up in a rural area. "Oh, those are worms that are mighty tasty to catfish. You have to dig deep to find them, though. The bigger, the better."

Josh poked his head out. "I tried digging there, but there weren't any."

"Guess I'll need to look somewhere else." Abandoning the toy shovel, Abram dusted off his hands. "You know a good place to dig?"

Josh shook his head. "No."

"Worms like damp, dark places." He pointed toward the landscaping stones lining the flower beds. "I bet if we look under those, we could find some."

Curious, Josh crawled out of the doghouse. Big for his age, he was all gangly limbs. By the look of him, he was going to be a tall man when he finally finished growing. With a shag of brown hair and brown eyes, he bore only a passing resemblance to his mother. He clearly took after his *daed.*

"You think it would be okay if we moved them?"

"We'll put them back when we're done."

Josh hovered by the doghouse like a nervous rabbit ready to bolt. "I don't want to get in any more trouble. Mrs. Graff is already mad at me."

"I heard about that. She's talking to your mom now."

Anxious, Josh glanced toward the house. "Is Mom real mad?"

"Not mad. More like disappointed, I think."

"I didn't mean to do anything bad," he said, kicking aimlessly at the dirt beneath his feet.

Judging by Josh's body language, he was clearly an unhappy *kind.* The *boi* was trying to adapt to a new way of life in a new state. He'd lost the support system of school, friends and the activities Maddie arranged to keep him engaged while she tried to make a living. No wonder they both felt overwhelmed. Everything they'd left behind would have to be rebuilt from scratch. Breaking the eggs had given the child a sense of control. Now, he had to deal with the remorse from his actions.

Josh knew he'd done wrong. He just didn't know how to make it right. Learning to control his anger and his impulses would be a big step in the right direction.

Abram blew out a breath. There was a time when he'd stood in Josh's shoes. He had been an obstinate *youngie*, too. And if there was trouble to be found, he was sure to find it. His own *daed* had had no patience with him and would rather punish him than talk to him.

He placed a hand against the pocket where his Bible rested. Since returning to the Amish church, he always carried it with him. Determined to lead a Christian life that was both productive and helpful, he liked having it close at hand to check the Lord's teachings when he was in doubt.

The good book instructed parents not to provoke children to anger but bring them up in the discipline and instruction of the Lord.

The boi doesn't need judgment, he thought. *He needs guidance.*

Josh had had enough time to think about what he'd done wrong. Now, he needed advice on how to correct his mistake.

Abram walked to the edge of a flower bed

and nudged over a heavy stone. A knot of fat worms wriggled in the rich, damp soil.

"Looks like we got some fine wigglers here. Why don't you get one of those buckets to keep 'em in?"

After a minute's hesitation, Josh complied. He dropped to his knees and poked at the writhing mass. "Oh, those are big ones."

Abram picked up a fat earthworm. "Now there's one the catfish will really like." Adding it to the pail, he dropped in a few more.

Josh wrinkled his nose. "Those don't look like they taste very good."

"If you're a fish, I suppose they're quite tasty."

Josh stuck out his tongue. "I'm glad I don't eat worms. I like pizza best."

"I think most everyone likes a good slice of pizza," Abram agreed. "You ever get to go fishing in Philadelphia?"

"No." Josh dropped more worms in the pail. "Sometimes Mom would make a picnic basket and we would go to the zoo or to the park. I liked that."

"But you didn't get to go very often?"

Josh blew out a frustrated breath. "Mom was always tired. And on the weekends, she had her sewing to do. She did alter—alternations for people's clothes."

"Alterations," Abram corrected.

"Yeah."

Abram tucked the information away. From the bits he'd picked up through conversation, he'd gleaned that life hadn't been easy for either of them the last few years. It sounded like Maddie had had to work seven days a week to keep their heads above water. He'd noticed that while Josh wore store-bought kid's clothes, his mother's dresses were made from scratch. She obviously put the *boi* first.

Sympathy squeezed hard. "Sounds like your mom worked hard to keep the bills paid."

"She does." The boy lowered his head. "Mrs. Graff said she would have to pay for the eggs."

Abram turned over another stone. More worms appeared. "Do you think that's fair?"

Fat tears rimmed Josh's eyes. "N-no, it's not. I shouldn't have done it." He swiped them away with an angry hand. "I'm sorry I got mad."

"Feeling sorry for what you did doesn't make things better. You must show people you want to do right. That's what a man does. He takes responsibility."

"B-but I'm just a kid."

"You're old enough to know right from wrong. How did you feel after you broke the eggs?"

Josh crinkled his nose. "I felt bad."

"Part of growing up is making amends. What you did hurt Mrs. Graff. And it hurt your mom. She works hard to provide the things you need."

Josh thought a moment. "If I had money, I'd pay for the eggs."

"Sounds like you want to take responsibility for what you did."

Sniffing, Josh wiped his nose on his sleeve. "I want to." His face took on a pensive expression. "But I don't know how to get any money."

Abram chuckled. Had he been born Amish, Josh would have been set to work when he was knee-high to a grasshopper. Amish children grew up learning their skill or trade from their parents. Young boys began an apprenticeship alongside their fathers or an older male relative as soon as they were old enough to walk and talk. Because Amish families were usually large, each member had a responsibility to contribute. Learning to be independent, yet still having the support of church and community, was a priceless advantage, one he felt many *Englisch* children missed out on. As a *youngie*, he hadn't appreciated being Amish. It was only after he'd departed Humble that he learned the true value of Plain folks.

"Well, to make money, you need a job."

Josh sniffled again. "Could I get one?"

Abram turned the question over in his mind. "Why don't we talk to your mom and see what she says? Maybe we can figure out something for you to do."

Sitting on Mrs. Graff's side porch, Maddie rested her head in her hands. Her nerves were twisted into knots. She was tired. Tired of the struggle. Tired of being broke. Just exhausted and worn to the bone.

Lifting her head, she glanced toward the faraway horizon. The sun had turned into a sliver, disappearing beneath the edge of the earth as night began to unfurl its velvet cloak.

The beauty of the moment touched her, a reminder that even in moments of despair, *Gott* was still in control of heaven and earth.

She gazed into the distance. "What am I doing wrong, Lord?"

In the back of her mind, the answer beckoned.

The lie.

She was living a lie. And no matter the justifications or excuses she offered, nothing would change the fact. The Bible clearly said he that speaketh lies shall perish.

Maddie's vision misted, though she refused to let a single tear fall. She'd had enough of crying, enough of feeling like a weak, stupid fool.

I need to get back in church. And I need to find a way to tell the truth about Josh.

Until that happened, she knew she would have no peace. Here she was, smack-dab in the middle of Amish country, walking amid people whose belief in *Gott* and His goodness was the bedrock of their community. It was why they chose to live the way they did, cutting themselves off from the temptations of the world and its many evils. They lived modest lives, relying on their faith to get them through hard times.

The simplicity of her childhood beckoned.

Whenever she recalled the happier times of her life, each precious memory centered around her loving grandparents. It was at her *maummi*'s side that she'd learned to cook on a wood-burning stove, to make her own clothes and to treat an illness with natural remedies.

Nightly, her dear *opa* led them through their Bible studies by the light of an oil-burning lamp. Afterward, they would have a cup of hot chocolate while he read the *Budget* newspaper to catch up on Amish news around the country. Things like television or video games weren't allowed in their household. Entertainment was self-made—sewing on a needlepoint project, reading a book or doing crossword puzzles.

Restless, Maddie sighed. Though she wanted to go back to being Amish, she doubted she'd ever be allowed to rejoin the church. She was the daughter of a shunned woman. For that, she might be forgiven. But she doubted she'd be forgiven for her own deceptions. Wreathing them in good intentions didn't lessen the sin.

Lost in her thoughts, she jumped when the back gate opened.

Pushing away negative thoughts, she pasted on a smile. Looking every bit like a scolded pup, Josh's face was puffy. Abram walked beside him, bracing the child with a reassuring hand.

Seeing them together, Maddie felt a warm sensation inside. Josh normally didn't care for strangers, especially men, but he seemed to have taken a shine to Abram. And having several nieces and nephews, Abram obviously had experience in dealing with *youngies*.

"I think Josh has something to say to you." Abram urged him forward with a gentle nudge.

Composing herself, Maddie nodded. "Go ahead."

"I'm sorry for breaking Mrs. Graff's eggs." His voice warbled with regret.

She nodded. Josh's apology lessened the weight overwhelming her emotions. There was no reason to be angry or yell. What was done was done. She would pay Mrs. Graff for the eggs and do as her landlady requested. Finding a new sitter on short notice would be hard, but she had no choice.

Rising, she pulled him into a hug. "I forgive you," she whispered, bending to kiss the top of his head. Even as she did, a bittersweet ache crushed her spirit. Josh might not have been her natural-born child, but she loved him as deeply as if he were. The idea that she could lose custody of him to his father frightened her more than anything in the world.

"I won't do anything like that again." Josh's small body trembled. "I promise."

Stepping back, Maddie placed her hands on his shoulders. "Want to tell me why you got in the henhouse and broke those eggs?"

Josh scuffed the dirt with the toe of his tennis shoe. "I was just looking for something fun. All Mrs. Graff has are puzzles and books. I got so bored."

"And?"

Guilt crept across his face. "When she wasn't looking, I snuck outside to look at the chickens. I didn't mean to break the eggs. I thought it would be fun to throw one...and I just...did."

Maddie heaved a fortifying breath. The thrill of breaking something was a primitive impulse. As a hyperactive child, Josh often acted without thinking. He also could not sit still in a quiet environment and was constantly fidgeting. From his point of view, puzzles and books were boring.

"I know it's hard staying with a sitter all day,

but things will get better when school starts. There will be more for you to do."

He wrapped his arms around her waist. "I didn't mean to cause any trouble, Mom."

"I know, honey. We'll figure something out."

Wanetta pushed open the screen door. "I've got supper on the table if anyone cares to have a bite." To back up her words, the delicious aroma of beef stew drifted out.

Maddie's stomach rumbled, reminding her she hadn't had a bite to eat since her awkward lunch with Abram. At least the misunderstanding between them had been cleared up.

"Join us?" she asked. "We've kept you from your supper."

Abram checked his pocket watch. "My driver will be back to pick me up shortly. But I'll be glad to have a cup of coffee while I wait."

Going inside, Maddie settled Josh in a seat at the dining room table before taking a chair herself. Abram took an empty seat across from them. Finished with the meal, the other boarders had dispersed for the evening.

Mrs. Graff bustled around, serving with a deft hand. Thick slices of corn bread dripping with home-churned butter accompanied bowls of meaty stew swimming with potatoes, carrots and onions.

"You sure you don't want to have a bite, Abram?"

"It does look mighty good. Maybe just a small helping. To tide me over until I get home."

"Never knew a man who could resist my stew." Chuckling, Wanetta headed back into the kitchen and dished up a third bowl.

"How's Lavinia and the baby?" she asked, adding cutlery and a napkin to his place.

Abram spread the linen across his lap. "Sophie had a little fever, but she's better now. Thanks for asking."

"Tell her I hope she's able to make it to the quilting bee next Wednesday."

"I certainly will."

"I'm gonna pay for the eggs, Mrs. Graff," Josh announced.

Mouth puckering, Wanetta set her hands on her hips. "Are you now?"

"Yes, ma'am, I am." Josh bobbed his head. "And I'm sorry I was mean and yelled at you."

The older woman's expression softened. "That does my heart *gut*. I'm glad to see a young man stand up and take responsibility for his actions."

"A man's gotta do what a man's gotta do," Josh said, all seriousness.

Maddie vaguely recalled the line from an old Western she and Josh had watched. "Is that so?"

Josh sat up straighter. "I'm pretty big now,

you know. I can work, too. I'm going to get a job."

"Oh?" She shifted her gaze to Abram. "Where?"

He gave a guilty smile. "That's something I wanted to talk to you about."

She glanced from one to the other. "Okay. Spill it."

Determined to be in on the conversation, Wanetta folded her arms across her chest.

Abram shifted in his chair. "Why don't you bring Josh to work with you?"

Maddie blinked. "What do you mean, bring Josh to work with me?"

"Exactly what I said."

"But how can I do my job if I'm watching my kid?"

"Because he's going to be busy at the market," Abram countered. "I can use someone to help me pack and deliver orders."

A laugh of disbelief slipped out. "You really want a little boy under your feet all day?"

"Why not? I watch Hiram and Hershel all the time, and if I can handle those two tiny terrors, I think I can handle Josh," he countered in all seriousness. "And he's not going to be under my feet. He's going to be working. And he's going to be earning a fair wage, just like any other employee."

"And I can help pay for things, 'cause I'm old

enough to be 'sponsible now," Josh added, puffing out his chest.

Deeply touched, Maddie's vision misted. Whatever Abram had said to Josh had certainly made an impression.

"I couldn't take your money, honey," she said, dabbing her eyes. "Why don't you think about saving it? Then you can replace your broken tablet."

"Tablets are for babies," Josh pronounced seriously. "I think we should save up for a truck, like Elam has. A red one, with big tires."

She smiled. Quite a big ambition for a little boy. "First you'd better save the money, and then we'll think about the truck."

Josh grinned. "Okay!"

Maddie turned to her landlady. "What do you think?"

"I think it is a fine idea," Wanetta announced, sealing the deal with a firm nod. "It will be *gut* for the *kind* to learn the value of a dollar."

"And the bonus is..." Abram added. "By the end of the day, he'll be pooped."

Maddie had to laugh. "That's a plus, for sure."

Abram peered over the rims of his glasses. "Then it's settled?"

Leaning back in her chair, Maddie considered his proposition. Not half an hour ago, she'd been feeling as if everything in her life was falling apart. Once again, Abram had presented a reasonable solution.

"I guess you will see both of us at the market tomorrow," she agreed, and then added a bit of caution. "I just hope you know what you're getting yourself into."

"Just give it a chance. It'll be fine. You'll see."

"Food's getting cold," Mrs. Graff reminded. Bustling back into her kitchen, she began to tidy up after the evening meal.

"Better get this eaten before my driver comes back." Abram steepled his hands and lowered his head, preparing to say grace. Following his example, Josh went quiet.

Bowing her head, Maddie couldn't resist peeking across the table. It humbled her to see a strong man giving sincere thanks to his savior. She'd only known Abram Mueller a few days, but it felt like they'd been friends for years. Sitting at the table, sharing a meal gave her a sense of place and security.

It was time to stop second-guessing her decision. Humble was home now, and it was where they would be staying.

A sense of relief filled her. The oppressive burden of defeat had lifted, replaced by hope.

Her roller-coaster day had come to an end, and everything had worked out.

Just the way *Gott* intended.

Closing her eyes, Maddie sent up a prayer of her own.

Thank You for watching over me and Josh, Lord. And thank You for sending Abram into our lives. We are both truly blessed.

The clock was close to striking nine when Abram arrived home. Thanking his driver for working late, he made a mental note to add a bit more to his pay at the end of the week.

The warm glow of oil-burning lamps emanated through the windows of the old house he shared with his *groossdaadi*. Passing through the gate, he walked up the cobbled path. Solar-powered garden lights lit the walkway and dotted the yard with pops of illumination.

He sat down at the foot of the stairs. Tipping back his head, he studied the stars scattered across soft folds of black velvet. Rising early, the moon was climbing in the sky toward its peak illumination. The wind was warm, just breezy enough to ruffle his hair where it stuck out beneath the brim of his straw hat. The beauty of the night offered peace and a time to reflect.

From his vantage point, he could see the other homes dotting the landscape. Most every one of his siblings had built a house on the property and was busy with the task of raising their *youngies*.

A frown pulled his mouth down. Everyone else was living their lives.

Me? I'm just existing.

He hadn't built a house on his share of the acreage because he'd never been able to envision himself as a married man with *kinder*. A bachelor like himself didn't need a house, so he'd let the land sit fallow, untouched and uncultivated.

Truth be told, he hadn't intended to stay in Humble. But after spending many years living in Milwaukee, he'd discovered he missed the simplicity of Amish living. He enjoyed getting up early and putting in a hard day's work. In the evenings, he spent an hour studying his Bible. After giving some time to the Lord, he worked around the property, making the repairs that would keep the house in good shape. His *familie* was also a large one, and he was often pressed into helping a sibling with a building project or monitoring his many nieces and nephews.

All in all, his was a satisfactory life. But it wasn't a joyful one. He went to bed alone at night and woke up the same way. And though he was trying to be patient, he'd wondered if *Gott* ever intended for him to have a wife.

Meeting Maddie Baum had added a splash of color to his drab days. Physically, she was a petite woman. But there was a lot of determination and drive packed into her tiny frame. Without the support of relatives or her child's father, she had a hard row to hoe. It pained him to think of her, alone and struggling. The world often wasn't kind to gentle souls.

Despite the hard lessons life had handed her, it hadn't taken away her ability to smile. She smiled often, and with a sincerity mirrored in the depths of her sparkling eyes. When she smiled, it was the real deal. Visiting with her turned his gray day into pure delight. It didn't matter what they were talking about. He was happy to have her attention.

The screen door creaked open. "Abram?"

Startled, he straightened. "Yes, Gran'pa?"

Leaning against his cane, Amos Mueller peeked out. "I was wondering when you'd make it home."

"I'm sorry I wasn't here. You've had supper, *ja*?"

"Lavinia served pinto beans and corn bread," Amos said through a grumble. "If only that girl would learn to cook. The beans were half-done and the corn bread too salty."

Abram chuckled. Even though her intentions were good, his younger sister's cooking wasn't. Boiling water for an egg often turned into a recipe for disaster.

"I take it you'd like to eat?"

"*Ja*, I'm peckish."

He took the hint. "I'll fix you some supper."

"About time." Happy to have the attention, the older man shuffled back inside.

Abram hung his hat on the peg by the door. Stepping inside was like traveling a century or more back in time. Glancing around, he took in the wood-burning stove, old-fashioned icebox and other items populating the large, open living space. The appliances were woefully out of date, but his *groossdaadi* refused to allow him to install anything propane or solar powered. Oil-burning lamps provided a familiar warmth.

Snagging a metal pot, he filled it with water from the spigot overhanging the basin. Pumped straight from the well, the water was ice-cold. As the house had no water heater, it made for a mighty uncomfortable bathing experience during the winter. As much as he tried, he couldn't change the elderly man's mind about updating a few things. Stubborn as a barnyard mule, Amos was determined to keep the modern world and its devices out of his home.

"Scrambled eggs with toast sound good?" he asked, stoking the fire with wood before setting the pot on to boil. His cooking skills weren't top-notch, but he could manage the basics.

Plopping down in his rocking chair, Amos

set his cane aside. "Breakfast for dinner sounds fine. Think you could throw on a slice of meat?"

"Sure can." Heading to the icebox, Abram gathered a couple of eggs and a slab of ham wrapped in wax paper, along with a few other items.

"How come you were late?"

"I was helping a friend. Maddie had a problem with her little *boi*."

"That girl... Didn't you have lunch with her today?" Amos asked, peevish. "You know I don't approve of her. She's an *Englischer*."

"Good thing it's not your decision." Cracking a couple of eggs into a bowl, he whipped them into a froth before adding some salt and pepper and a pat of butter. Letting the mix rest, he took down a cast iron skillet and set it on the stovetop to heat before slicing off a few pieces of ham to fry.

The old man scratched his chin. Though widowed quite a few years, he'd kept his bushy beard, now grown halfway down his chest. Though the *Ordnung* allowed men to keep their facial hair neatly trimmed, it was another thing Amos Mueller considered impious and refused to do.

"You just ain't listening."

Abram stabbed the sizzling meat with a fork, giving it a quick turn. "I know what you think. But I'm a grown man. I'll pick my own friends." Transferring the fried ham to a plate, he poured the whipped eggs into the skillet. "Anyway, Maddie's *boi*—Josh is his name—he's giving her a little trouble. Stealing, getting into things, talking back."

The elderly man snuffled, something that sounded like half a laugh. "Sounds like you when you were that age."

"Yeah, it does."

Frowning, Abram scraped a spatula through the eggs to keep them from scalding. Talking with Josh was like visiting with the younger version of himself. The boy's frustrations and discontent simmered beneath the surface, ready to explode without warning.

Unbidden images unspooled across his mind's screen. A few months after his fourth birthday, his own *mamm* had passed away from a sudden virus. Barely three months after her funeral, his *daed* married Noemi Jaeger. Young and pretty, she'd moved in and set to erasing her predecessor's presence from the house. Soon, she was with child, and new *kinder* filled the nursery. In no time at all, Abram had four younger siblings. Before that, he'd been the baby—and his *mamm*'s favorite.

Noemi despised him.

And tormented him.

In retaliation, he'd turned into a *gor*, a brat.

Anything he could do to rebel against her rules, he would.

Abram grimaced. The more he angered his stepmother, the more his *daed* pulled out the strap. Then, he'd viewed the punishments as a badge of honor. The older he got, the more stubborn he became. In his mind, he knew everything, and his elders knew nothing.

But he wasn't as clever as he believed.

And his disobedience had cost two of his friends their lives.

Hands shaking a bit, he forced himself to concentrate on his cooking. Eggs done, he scraped them onto the plate. Slicing a couple of pieces of bread, he added a smear of butter before toasting them in the skillet. Food done, he grabbed some cutlery and a linen napkin before carrying it to the table.

"Food's ready," he said, deciding it was best to change the subject.

The past, like his parents, was gone. Both Noemi and his *daed* had been killed in a buggy accident years ago. The house he'd grown up in had been razed to the ground.

Rising, Amos shuffled to the table. "Better than what Lavinia served."

"Glad you think so." Spooning instant coffee and a dash of sugar into a mug, he added hot water. He normally didn't drink anything caffeinated in the evening, but there was no way he'd ever get to sleep. He had too much on his mind.

Amos cut into the ham, fumbling with his knife. "My old hands," he complained. "Don't work right anymore with this arthritis."

Setting his coffee down, Abram cut the meat into manageable pieces. "Better?"

"Mmm-hmm..." The old man dug into his food, tearing his toast to scrape up his eggs, followed by bites of ham.

Descending into silence, Abram sipped his coffee. He just wanted to sit and enjoy the silence.

"You made nothing for yourself," his grandfather commented. Usually, they ate their evening meal together. Afterward, Abram would read from the Bible or another approved publication until the old man fell asleep.

"Had something at Wanetta's place. She served up a nice beef stew."

"Runs that boardinghouse, doesn't she?"

"Yes. Maddie is renting her loft."

"That *fraulein*—Maddie, you say—you like her?"

He shrugged. "I suppose I do."

Suspicion crept into Amos Mueller's expression. "Would you leave the faith for her?"

Caught by surprise, Abram lowered his mug. Abandoning his faith would mean automatic excommunication. His name would be announced to the entire Plain community, and he would go under the *bann*. No one would be allowed to have a meal or ride in a buggy with him. All socialization was discouraged, implemented to teach the offender a lesson they wouldn't forget.

"Are you questioning my commitment to the church because I spent a few hours helping Maddie with her *sohn*?"

Finishing his last bite, Amos pushed the empty plate away. "You've left the faith before because you were lured by *Englisch* ways."

Abram frowned. "I was unbaptized."

The old man doubled down. "But you are baptized now. And it's not proper for an unwed Amish man and a single *Englisch* woman to spend time together. You have no business visiting her."

Abram forced himself not to roll his eyes. His *groossdaadi* was a stickler for the old ways and felt a man should not even be seen speaking in a familiar way to any female who was not accompanied by her *ehmann* or her *daed*, should she be unmarried. As for *Englisch* women—they were strictly off-limits in every way.

"Gran'pa, bless your soul. I've done nothing scandalous. And I don't intend to."

A squint crossed the table. "I don't want you seeing her again."

Abram gathered his patience. "That's not sensible. Maddie works at the market. I've no good reason to let her go."

Amos wiped his mouth with his thumb and forefinger before brushing away the crumbs in his beard. "Fine. Just don't go getting too fond of her. She doesn't belong in this *familie*."

Swallowing against the emotion tightening his throat, Abram drained his mug. "Maddie's just a friend," he said after a moment's silence. "Nothing more."

Chapter Seven

"What are we going to be today?"

Hand nestled in her larger one, Josh glanced up. "Respectful, mindful and grateful," he said, repeating back the morning's lesson.

"Very good."

Guiding him toward the Amish market, Maddie felt her nerves tighten. When Abram had suggested that she bring Josh to work with her, she'd thought he might be joking. But as their conversation had progressed, it had seemed like the best solution to the problem.

Asking Mrs. Graff to give him another chance wasn't an attractive option. The dilemma with Josh would still be the same—he was hyperactive and had a short attention span. Finding a day care might be doable, but it would take time to find the right place she could afford. Because they'd left Philadelphia on short notice, she also didn't have any of Josh's recent school or medical records. Even though she'd asked her former landlord to forward her mail, it could take a while for the paperwork she needed to show up. Her only option was to give Abram's suggestion a try.

"Now remember, mind your elders, and if you feel yourself getting mad, stop and take deep breaths."

"I'm a working man now," Josh said, clutching the lunch box Mrs. Graff had packed.

"Yes. You are. And I'm so proud."

As they walked, the rest of the employees gave them a few stares but said nothing. A little less reserved, a few of the younger women smiled.

"*Guten morgen*, Maddie," Gretl greeted as they joined the others and walked inside.

"*Guten morgen*," Maddie returned. Living around other people who spoke the language daily had prodded her into remembering a lot of what she'd forgotten. Switching from *Englisch* to *Deitsch* was getting easier.

"And who is this *kleiner*?"

"This is my *sohn*, Josh," she explained. "I've lost my sitter, so Abram said I could bring him to work. He's going to be helping him with deliveries."

"Good morning, ma'am," Josh said politely.

"*Ach*, good morning, little one."

Pleased with his manners, Maddie directed Josh to put his lunch box in the fridge. "I'll be there in a minute," she said, reaching for her time card.

"I think that's wonderful," Gretl continued, taking care of her own. "Abram's *gut* about helping mothers when they need a hand with their *youngies*. You are not the first *mutter* who has had to bring her *kinder* to work."

"I'm relieved to know that."

Glancing around, Gretl leaned close. "It's true. When Juanita Trent's *ehmann* up and left, she had to bring her two babes for several months. She's an *Englischer*, and her no-good man left her without a cent. *Gott* bless him, Abram helped her out with extra food and baby things until her *familie* could move her."

Though she never indulged in idle gossip, Maddie wasn't surprised Abram had stepped up to help.

"I feel blessed to know him."

"To know who?" a familiar voice inquired from behind.

Maddie pivoted. Abram stood a few feet behind her, a bemused look on his face. Unlike many Amish men who wore their hair in the traditional bowl cuts, his collar-length mane of black curls tumbled aimlessly across his forehead. His glasses gave him a studious air but failed to dim the sparkle in his eyes.

Embarrassed, her stomach did a slow backflip. A ribbon of warm familiarity wound itself through her.

"Um, you. I said, I'm blessed to know *you*."

A smile spread across his face. "I'm glad you feel that way. *Danke* for the kind thoughts."

"*Bitte*," Maddie answered, dropping her gaze. "I'm grateful you let me bring Josh."

Looking between the two of them, Gretl threw out a quick "See you later." She scurried away before she got a scolding for wagging her tongue.

Abram placed his hands on his hips. Dressed in a pair of broadfall trousers and a white shirt covered with a heavy-duty denim apron, he was ready for work. "Where's my helper for the day?"

Josh bounded up, standing on the tips of his toes to make himself taller. "I'm right here."

Abram smiled down at him. "I'm glad you made it. We're going to have a busy day, you and me."

Josh looked at the rest of the employees waiting their turn to clock in. "Do I get to have a card, too?"

"Why, of course."

Plucking one from a nearby stack, he gave Josh

a pen and showed him where to write his name. That done, he lifted the boy up and instructed him how to insert the card to be stamped.

Josh proudly added his card to the rack. "I'm a working man now," he announced to the group.

A few of the younger clerks laughed and gave him the thumbs-up.

"Yes, you are," Maddie said, pushing stray bangs away from his forehead.

Leaving the break room, they walked down to the short hallway toward her office. "Are you sure he's not going to be too much trouble?"

"I'll keep him busy. If he gets tired, we can put a cot in your office. The phone shouldn't disturb him if you set the ringer to low and wear a headset."

"Naps are for babies," Josh said, butting in.

"He's never been a kid that napped," Maddie explained. "In day care and kindergarten, he drove his teachers crazy because they couldn't get him to sleep. He's always been like the Energizer Bunny. Going and going and going."

"Sounds like I'll be the one needing a nap."

"Most likely, you will. He will run circles around you."

"Well, I'm only thirty, so I think I can keep up," Abram gave her a wink. "At least, I hope I can."

Maddie pulled up and printed the orders that

had come in overnight by email from their *Englisch* customers. Just as the clock struck eight, the phone began to ring. She reached for her headset. The day was going to be a busy one.

"Here you go," she said, handing over the stack. "I'll get these processed for billing as soon as I can."

He thumbed through the stack. "Looks like we're really picking up. Might have to think about getting another buggy and driver if this keeps up."

Josh's little face lit up with delight. "We get to ride in a buggy?"

"Sure do."

Maddie grinned. Josh found the ideas of horses and buggies fascinating and loved riding in one. As a kid raised in a city setting, his closest contact with large animals was at the zoo. Even though she would have liked to have had a dog, or even a cat, most of the complexes where they rented didn't allow pets. The best she could ever manage was a goldfish. Often, the poor thing died within a few weeks, prompting another trip to the pet store.

"By the time you spend all day in one, you'll be tired of looking at a horse's rear end."

"When I'm bigger, I'm gonna learn to drive one," Josh decided then and there.

"Sounds good to me." Abram checked his

watch. "I guess we'd better get busy if we're going to get these orders filled."

The two departed to tackle their busy day. Abram was tall, and his stride was wide. Josh had to double his steps to keep up. Chattering without a single breath between words, he practically bounced with joy.

Drawing a breath to steady her nerves, she watched them go.

If only Josh had a proper daed, she thought. *Abram would be perfect.*

Blinking hard, she gave her head a shake.

Now where had that idea come from?

A bitter ache crept through her, circling her heart with a vicious grip. Fresh tears stung her eyes. She hadn't realized how much she missed being Amish until she'd moved back to Humble. But living under a veil of deceit meant she would never be able to return to the Plain community.

Her facade of calm began to crumble. The cracks in her psyche were growing wider. Soon, she wouldn't be able to plaster over them.

Closing the door to her office, Maddie took a seat at her desk. The phone kept up its incessant ringing, but she couldn't bear to pick up the receiver. Instead, she leaned forward and pressed her forehead against her steepled hands.

Lord, help me make things right. I can't live this lie much longer.

* * *

Loading the days' deliveries, Abram checked to make sure everything was correctly labeled for the customers. Giving his horse a quick pat on the rump, he glanced down at Josh.

"Ready to go?"

Josh nodded eagerly. "Yes, sir."

Abram slid open the door to the cab. "Up you go."

Josh scrambled into the enclosed space, settling onto the wide, padded seat. Taking in the details, his eyes grew wide. "Wow, it's like a spaceship in here."

Climbing in, Abram chuckled. A glance at the dash revealed a speedometer and a GPS, LED lighting, and many other features one might expect to find in a car. There was even a switch for turn signals. On the outside were lights and other safety features for traveling after dark, all battery powered. Unlike most buggies, which were simple and utilitarian, the one used for grocery deliveries had been specially designed with a van-style insulated storage. Created out of thermally modified wood, it was waterproof and rot resistant.

"Pretty fancy, eh?"

"It's cool. I like it."

Abram chuckled. "I do, too."

Guiding the buggy out into the street, Abram

let the horse set its pace. Settling back to enjoy the ride, he glanced at Josh.

Throughout the morning the *boi* had worked tirelessly, running back and forth to help the clerks gather the groceries on their lists. Afterward, Josh helped bag the items, meticulously arranging items by size and shape. Once that task was completed, he'd carried some of the less heavy parcels to be loaded for delivery. Doing as he was told, he hadn't complained a single time about being tired or bored.

Lulled by the steady *clip-clop* of the horse's hooves on the pavement, Abram's thoughts turned to the conversation he'd had with his *groossdaadi*. While Abram didn't believe he was doing anything wrong, Amos seemed to believe he was in danger of being lured away from the faith.

Lips going flat, he shook his head. Did Amos really believe he was that foolish?

Yes, he wanted a wife. And, yes, he believed Maddie would be a wonderful helpmate.

But he was also aware there was a line he couldn't cross—unless she rejoined the church.

As it stood, he had no inkling about her thoughts on the matter. Were she to choose to return, she would be required to undergo a rigorous interview with the bishop. And then there would be weeks of intense counseling to reacquaint her with the teachings of the church and reaffirm her commitment to *Gott.*

It wasn't a straightforward process. And it wasn't always the right choice for everyone.

He'd known a couple of people who'd backtracked when their day of baptism came around. The bishop gave every man and woman the chance to change their minds. Once the ceremony was complete, a person was expected to remain committed to the church throughout their lifetime.

Abram hadn't been sure he wanted to stay in the community after coming of age. His stepmother was a source of irritation, and his *daed* didn't have a friendly word to say about him.

After the accident that had scarred his face, his *daed* had disowned him. His paternal grandparents had to take him in. Amos put him to work in the market, guiding him the same way he was trying to guide Josh. He'd also taken an apprenticeship in carpentry to give him a solid skill set and enable him to find work should he decide shopkeeping wasn't what he wanted to do. His grandparents, though distant and taciturn, had provided him with a solid foundation as he grew from an angry adolescent into a calmer, more focused adult.

The shrill blare of a truck horn cut through

the snarl in his mind, reminding him to pay attention to his driving.

He glanced at Josh. The kid was a ball of energy, all bright-eyed and bushy-tailed. "How are you holding up?"

"I really like the market. It's a fun place to be."

"I'm glad you think so."

"It would be so great if Zach and Bobby could be here."

"Those are your buddies?"

"Uh-huh. We played together at school."

"Must be hard, leaving your friends behind to move to a new place."

A shrug rolled off Josh's small shoulders. "I'm used to moving around," he confessed. "Once, Mom lost her job and we had to live in a shelter. You could only stay a month, and then you had to go somewhere else. We lived in the car when they said we couldn't stay there anymore."

Though he'd suspected Maddie and Josh had been through hard times, learning they had been homeless tugged at his heartstrings. By the sound of things, Maddie had fought a tough battle to keep ahead of poverty. He couldn't imagine not having a roof over his head. No matter how far away he might have gone, he always had the security of *familie* to help in a pinch.

Her courage and determination only increased his admiration.

"What did you think of that?" Like most children, Josh was a fount of information.

"I kind of liked it. It was like camping out. We would stay in places like rest stops and parks. Then Mom got a job working for Mr. Cohen and got some money to rent a place in Brewerytown." His nose wrinkled. "Mom didn't like it there. She said it was dangerous."

"Did Mr. Cohen own the dry cleaner where your mom worked?"

"Yeah. Mr. Cohen was nice and always gave us *schnecken*. That's kind of like cinnamon rolls with raisins. They were good." Pausing a moment, he added, "He always wore a little round hat, like a circle on his head. He had a beard, too, like some guys here have. And he sometimes said funny words, like everyone here does." He gave his head a scratch. "Mom knows what people are saying, but I don't."

Suspecting Maddie's former employer to be an Orthodox Jew who probably spoke Yiddish, Abram chuckled. Amish men also had beards but grew no mustaches under their noses. And the *Deitsch* language did sound strange to those unaccustomed to hearing it daily.

"For Amish men, a beard means they are married."

"Oh. That's good, I guess. So, you're not married?"

"No. Not yet. I hope to be. Someday."

"My mom's not married, either." Josh gave a hopeful look. "Maybe you could marry her. She needs someone."

"Why do you think that?"

"Well, she's always alone, except for me. And she has to do everything by herself." Josh's small face took on shadows of sadness. "Sometimes, she cries. She thinks I don't know, 'cause she thinks I'm asleep. I feel bad, and I cry, too."

Hands tightening on the reins, Abram cut his gaze away. Though he hadn't known Maddie long, the attraction he felt was undeniable. There was something special about her, something that set her apart from other women.

"I'm sorry your mom is sad. But I can't marry her, because she's not Amish."

"Then you should tell her to be," Josh said, as if it were that simple.

"As much as I would like to, it doesn't quite work that way. To be Amish, your mom would have to live in the faith and abide by the rules of the *Ordnung*."

Making a face, Josh twisted his tongue around the strange word. "What's an *ord*—what you said?"

"The *Ordnung*. It's a set of rules. Kind of like the Ten Commandments in the Bible."

"You mean, like, don't steal things or tell lies?"

"Yes, like that. And it's why we don't have things like electricity in our homes. We're willing to live a simpler life because we believe it helps keep us close to *Gott* and doesn't tempt us into sin."

"Elam has a truck. Does that mean he's a sinner?"

"It's different for Elam because he isn't baptized in the faith," he explained gently. "Elam hasn't yet made his commitment to *Gott*. He can live like the *Englisch* if he wants to."

"What's that word mean?"

"That's what the Amish call people outside the church. You and your mom are *Englisch*."

"Oh. Okay." Gaze narrowing, Josh thought a minute. "I don't think I want to be Amish," he finally announced. "It sounds really hard. I don't understand a lot of the words or why it's bad to have things we want."

"Wanting things doesn't mean you're bad. The Amish look at things a little differently. Some items we think are necessary, and some items we don't believe we have a need for."

Josh scratched his head. "All these rules are pretty confusing."

"Plain folks are just different. Your mom was Amish, and she might want to be again, someday."

His eyes widened. "Really? I didn't know that."

"It's true. She told me so herself. That means you could choose to be, too, when you grow up."

"I'll be eight soon." He sat up straighter. "That's pretty grown-up."

Abram chuckled. "You still have a few years to go."

Leaning back against the seat, Josh kicked aimlessly at the footboard. His discontent was apparent. "I guess."

"If you will give it some time, I think you'll like living in Humble. It's not what you're used to, but new experiences in life help us grow and understand other people better."

"I like being at the market and stuff like that. But…"

"What?"

"Nothing. Mom says *Gott*—that's what she calls God—will give us what we're supposed to have, when we're supposed to have it." A look of longing came into his gaze. "I sure wish God would hurry up sometimes."

"Sounds like you've been waiting for something for a long time."

Gaze swimming with fathomless longing,

Josh lowered his head. "I don't think God answers prayers," he mumbled. "I ask, but I never get anything."

Sympathy twisted Abram's insides. "It's not in the asking," he explained gently. "It's in the receiving. *Gott* knows what you need. Believe me, it's true. He's just waiting for the right time to send it."

Josh swiped at his eyes. "But when?"

"That's part of faith," he said, carefully measuring each word. "Trusting that the Lord knows what He's doing."

Josh thought a moment. "Maybe God can't hear me because Heaven's real far away," he reasoned. "I'll ask louder."

Abram hid a chuckle behind his hand. In a *youngie*'s mind, that would make perfect sense. "*Gott*'s listening. Just give Him a chance to put things in order. He will. Just you wait and see."

Chapter Eight

By the time Saturday evening came around, Maddie was ready for a break. The week had been a long one, but satisfying. Though parts of her job were overwhelming at first, she'd quickly gotten the hang of it. She liked the work and embraced the new friendships she was building with coworkers.

Josh also seemed to enjoy the time he spent at the market. The other employees had taken him under their wing, helping to keep him focused and busy. To help him fit in, one of the girls had sewn him a miniature version of the aprons the clerks wore as part of their uniform. Josh wore it with pride, carefully hanging it up each night.

Saturday was also payday. And while a check was issued for her wages, Abram had given Josh cash. With great care, he'd counted out the amount they'd agreed on—ten dollars. Along with the tips he'd earned, he was doing very well.

Proud of his accomplishment, he'd dutifully paid Mrs. Graff for the eggs he'd broken. "I earned this," he said, pulling the bills and loose change out of his pocket. "All by myself." He carefully counted out three dollars.

Wanetta accepted payment. "*Danke*, young man," she said, tucking the money away. "I appreciate that you've paid for the damage. I hope you've learned a lesson."

Standing a little straighter, Josh puffed out his chest. "I'm taking care of business, like a 'sponsible man should."

Proud, Maddie ruffled his hair. "Well, you're not quite a grown-up yet. But I'm proud of you."

Abram's solution was spot-on. Josh hadn't had one episode for the last four days. Up early, he was exhausted by the time they got home. His head usually hit his pillow soon after supper. They'd agreed he would stay on the schedule until it was time to start school. After that he'd continue part-time, helping in the afternoons.

"Can we order a pizza?" He held out the rest of his wadded cash. "I can pay for it."

She looked at him, impressed by his generosity. Josh could be such a good kid when he was given the chance. His hyperactivity made it hard for him to focus, but when he had a place to channel his energy, he did fine. By helping at the market, he wasn't only learning to pay attention and follow directions, he was learning the value of a day's work. When they'd arrived in Humble, he'd been sulky and destructive. Under a firm hand, his attitude had completely turned around.

Touched by his offer, she gazed at his eager face. He deserved a reward. An evening of pizza and board games would be a fine way to spend time together. "I don't see why not. But you can keep what you earned. I'll pay."

He tucked his money away. "I'm gonna put this in my piggy bank. For a 'mergency."

She rewarded him with a smile. "Sounds good. But let's hope we don't have any." She pointed toward the stairs leading to their loft. "Why don't you go wash your face and change clothes while I walk down to the phone box and order a pizza?"

"Yay!" Josh disappeared up the stairs.

Wanetta watched him go. "I've never seen such a change in a *youngie* before. When you got here, he was so sullen. Now, he's all smiles."

Maddie slipped off her work sweater, hanging it on a peg by the back door. "Working at the market has been good for him. He loves riding in the buggy and making the deliveries."

"Sounds like Abram has become a father figure of sorts." The older woman arched a brow. "He'd make a good *ehmann*, too, I think." Wanetta was known for speaking her mind. She didn't care what others thought. If she had something to say, she'd say it.

"I am sure he will make some lucky woman a fine spouse," she countered, brushing off the comment. "But I don't ever plan to marry, at all."

Wanetta gave her a knowing look. "I saw how Abram looked at you the other night when he was sitting here. He's sweet on you, no doubt in my mind."

Maddie blushed, feeling heat creep into her cheeks. Her heart beat a little faster, quickening her pulse. Since they'd met, Abram had occupied a significant portion of her thoughts. She liked him. A lot. There were not enough words to describe his generosity and kindness. And if she were to admit the truth, she'd even daydreamed a little about what it might be like to be his wife.

"Oh, please. Don't say that. It's not even possible."

"You say you're not interested, but I think you are." She eyed Maddie from head to foot. "What I see standing in front of me is a Plain woman, through and through. It's the reason I decided to rent to you. And I think it's just a matter of time before you are called back to the faith. And then I've no doubt you'll marry Abram. Just you wait and mark my words. You'll see."

Maddie drew in a breath and then let it out slowly. "I don't know if the church would have me back," she confessed.

"I think *Gott* has plans for you." Giving her a narrow look, Wanetta crossed her arms. "You may not think so, but I know time will prove me right. You should speak with Bishop Graber. He is a *gut* man and has helped guide many members back to the community."

Mouth going dry, Maddie licked her lips. Talking with the bishop would mean she'd have to confess everything. And that would expose the fact that she'd lied to many people.

Though she'd once believed her deceit harmed no one and protected Josh from the tragedy in his past, she'd come to realize she was wrong. What had started out as a small rewrite of the facts had grown exponentially, tying up her conscience and putting her soul in a dangerous noose. She'd hanged herself with her own good intentions.

"I'll take your word for it. And I'll certainly give your suggestion about talking to the bishop due consideration." Ending the conversation, she stepped away. "Now, if you'll excuse me, I'm going to walk down and order a pizza."

Like most Amish folks, Wanetta didn't have a landline in her home, nor did she use a cell phone. However, many of the older neighborhoods shared a common phone, usually kept in a shack located within walking distance. This allowed residents to communicate without breaking the rules of the *Ordnung*.

Swiping a dish rag across an already immaculate counter, her landlady nodded. "Sounds *gut*, dear."

A knock on the front door interrupted.

A frown wrinkling her brow, the older woman glanced up. "Now who could that be?"

"I'll get it." Leaving the kitchen, Maddie passed through the sprawling living room. She opened the door. Elam Mueller stood outside.

"Evening, ma'am." He doffed his cap. "Sorry to bother."

"No bother at all."

"Got something for you." Grinning, Elam turned and spread his arms toward the street. "Looks pretty good, don't you think?"

Stepping outside, Maddie gaped. Hooked behind Elam's big truck was her car. Abram waved from the pickup.

Jaw dropping, her eyes widened in disbelief. "What's this?"

"Your car's fixed and we're dropping it off," he explained.

"You repaired it in less than a week?"

His grin widened. "Sure did."

"Oh, my. This is wonderful!"

"Check it out."

Half disbelieving, she followed the cobblestone path through the front yard. Opening the gate, she stepped into the street. The station wagon sat on four new tires, complete with matching hubcaps.

Abram slid out of the passenger's seat. "Bet you weren't expecting to see it so soon."

"No. I wasn't." She pressed her hands to her mouth. "Oh, my. I think I'm going to cry. How did you do it?"

"My boss let me search through the salvage yard, and we found a wrecked one similar to your model," Elam explained. "He let me strip it down for what I needed. I hope that's okay. The parts aren't new, but they're solid. Couple of the fellas I work with helped me out, so the repairs went a little faster. We checked everything over to make sure it was safe."

"Why would I mind? I'm grateful you were able to get it running. I had a vision of it being hauled away for scrap metal."

"No chance of that. I know how it feels being without your wheels," Elam said. "It's like your legs have been cut off."

"I have to admit, it's tough being without a

car. It's so convenient to jump in when I want to go to the store or pick up something. I've had it so long it's almost a part of me."

Holding out a hand, Elam dangled the keys. "Here you go. It's ready to run."

Claiming them, Maddie slipped behind the wheel. Thoughtfully, the boys had taken the time to detail it. There wasn't a speck of dust to be found, inside or out. Pushing the key into the ignition, she gave it a twist. The lights came on and the engine roared to life, settling into a steady hum.

She cocked her head. "It's never sounded this good."

"All it needed was a little TLC and some elbow grease."

She killed the engine. "This is unbelievable. I can't thank you and your friends enough for all the work you did. Please, let me pay you."

Elam waved a dismissive hand. "You don't owe anything. I used the car as the project I needed to complete my certification. My boss at the shop supervised the work and signed off on it. I'll be a certified mechanic soon."

"I'm glad it helped you out." Maddie shook her head. "But those tires don't look used to me and must have cost you something."

Elam glanced at his older brother. "Abram paid for them," he said, walking around to unhook her car. Gathering the tow chains, he set them in the back of his truck. "How you settle it with him is his concern."

"Well, then I'll have to pay your brother."

Joining the conversation, Abram held up his hands. "Those bald things you were riding around on weren't safe. No way was I letting you go down the road until they were replaced."

She placed her hands on her hips, ready to argue her side. "And you'll tell me how much you paid and take the money," she countered, attempting a frown, and failing. "I'm not a charity project, Abram Mueller. I can take care of my obligations."

He backed down. "I'll accept payment," he said after giving it some thought. "But only if you agree to pay it out a little at a time."

"That's fair." Paying Abram back would make it clear that she wasn't going to let him step in and take care of her problems. It wasn't his place to do so.

"I was just about to order a pizza. Please, stay and let me treat you and Elam to a meal."

Abram shook his head. "Actually, we stopped by to see if you and Josh would like to go skating this evening. Hiram and Hershel are having their birthday celebration this weekend, and they wanted to go to the rink tonight as their big present."

Maddie's brow wrinkled. "Amish on roller skates?"

"Why not?" Gaze twinkling, Abram laughed. "It gives the *youngies* a chance to socialize, and it's good exercise for them."

The offer was tempting. An evening out in a family setting sounded like a wonderful break after a long and stressful week.

It didn't take long to decide.

"I think that's great idea. We're in. Josh will love it, I know." She glanced down at her work clothes. "I'll need a few minutes to change and get Josh ready. Do you mind waiting?"

Abram offered a boyish grin. "Sounds like a plan."

Maddie hurried inside, shutting the kitchen door behind her. "Plans have changed."

Wanetta glanced up. "I see your car is back."

"I can't believe Elam got it fixed so quickly."

"A true blessing."

Maddie smiled. "It is." She vaguely gestured toward the stairs leading to the loft. "We've been invited to go skating. I think Josh will enjoy it."

"I think he will, too." Tipping her head toward a small table near the foot of the stairs, Wanetta added, "I forgot to say there's mail for you. I've set it on the tray there."

"*Danke.*" Crossing the kitchen, she reached

for the stack. Having been in Humble such a brief time, she wasn't really expecting anything right away. The school secretary had told her not to look for Josh's records for at least a month. Nevertheless, her former landlord had promised to forward anything that came in until the change of address she'd registered at the post office kicked in.

Pausing at the foot of the stairs, she sorted through the envelopes. Most of it was junk, nothing important. Only the postcard with a view of a sun-drenched beach stood out.

Greetings From California, it read.

Maddie turned it over. The card was unsigned. There was no return address. The card had been sent to their old apartment in Philadelphia. The postmark showed it had been sent from Sacramento a few weeks ago.

Her breath drizzled away. Heart skipping a beat, she felt icy chips slash through her veins. She knew without a doubt who had sent it. The timing coincided with the date Cash was to be set free from prison.

Looking at the cheery card, she swallowed thickly. Leaving Philadelphia hadn't solved the problem. It had only delayed the inevitable.

Cash was coming, and trouble would be coming with him.

There was nowhere else to go. Nowhere else to hide.

She'd run as far as she could.

Wanetta sensed her discomfort. "Is everything all right?" she asked. "You went so pale."

Her jaw tightened. "I'm fine. It's nothing important."

"If you say so."

Anger surged through her. Without thinking twice, she ripped the card in half and tossed it in the trash can with the rest of the discarded mail.

I'm not going to let that man ruin our lives.

She was tired of living in fear. She'd been pushed far enough. It was time to stand up.

If Cash wanted a fight, she'd give him one.

On Saturday night, the roller rink was full. People of all ages came to enjoy the facility, filling it to maximum capacity.

The *kinder* were having a wonderful time, laughing and teasing each other. It also gave the adults a chance to unwind and catch up on visiting.

Skates rented, the *youngies* headed out onto the floor. Rather than blast modern pop music, the rink DJ played old-time country tunes to keep the participants moving. A mix of *Englisch* and Amish children sped around, some coming perilously close to colliding and going down in a heap. An adult supervisor made sure the trouble got toned down when some of the older boys started racing around the less experienced skaters.

Abram leaned against the rail, enjoying the time with his *familie*. Most of his brothers and sisters had come out for the evening. Only Rolf and his wife, Violet, were missing. Their infant, Hannah, was teething and feeling fussy. Their oldest daughter, Trisha, was keeping an eye on her younger brother, Henry. Annalise had bought Zeke and Eli, leaving her *ehmann* at home. Samuel's wife, Frannie, had also stayed home to get things ready for Hiram and Hershel's birthday party, which would take place Sunday evening after church.

He turned an ear toward the conversation. He was glad Maddie had agreed to join them, as it gave him a chance to spend time with her in a social setting. She stood, chatting with his younger siblings. He hoped, given time, they would come to like her as much as he did.

"*Ach*, those kids," Lavinia said, rolling her eyes. "Looks like I need to get out there and get them under control."

"You skate?" Maddie asked.

Lavinia grinned. "You bet I do." She looked at Josiah. "Remember when we were courting? We'd skate together holding hands."

Quiet and reserved, Josiah Simmons gave his young wife a shy look. “I sure do. I thought I’d have to spend forever on that rink to get you to marry me.”

Maddie smiled. “What a wonderful story.”

Annalise reached for Sophie. “I’ll hold her while you skate. Remind Zeke and Eli they’re to be careful. I don’t need another broken arm to deal with.”

Sitting on a nearby bench, Samuel slipped on his own skates. “Hiram and Hershel always want to race.” He glanced at Abram. “You skating tonight?”

Abram looked at Maddie. “Want to put on a pair?” He nodded toward the skate counter.

Waving her hands, Maddie shook her head. “I never learned. My grandparents were very strict as to what we could and could not do,” she explained. “Skating would have been scandalous to my *maummi*. And aside from singing in church, music wasn’t allowed.”

“You couldn’t even listen to the radio?”

“Nope. Not at all. *Opa* said silence was golden and gave us more time to reflect on the Lord.”

Lavinia gave her a look. “You never got to do anything?”

“There was always something to do,” Maddie replied. “*Maummi* made sure we were kept busy.

Idle hands were the devil's playground, she said. Cooking, cleaning, mending clothes—"

"Is all work," Annalise countered, cradling her niece in her arms. "But what did you do to enjoy yourselves?"

"Well, nothing like this. Maybe that's why I have such a hard time socializing. All I do is work and go home to take care of Josh. I've always tried to be responsible. Because I've always been afraid..."

"Afraid of what?" Lavinia prodded.

Maddie visibly tensed. "That he'd be taken away from me."

Her answer prodded Abram's curiosity. She had never mentioned Josh's father or the family the *kind* might have on his paternal side. From what he'd gleaned, she had no contact with the fellow, and Josh didn't know his *daed.*

"I don't think that's anything you'd ever have to fear," he said, joining in. "You're a good *mamm.* I've seen that with my own eyes."

Stepping to the rail circling the rink, Maddie gazed through the crowd. She seemed a little tense. Nervous. Laughing and shouting, Josh was playing roller tag with Hiram and Hershel and a few other boys. Her gaze softened as she watched him play. Despite her smile, sadness lingered in the depths of her gaze.

"I've done my best," she admitted. "But a lot of the time, I think it's not good enough."

"Josh is a fine, healthy boy," Samuel said, joining in. "I've seen how he acts at the market with my own eyes. He's smart and gets along with everyone. He follows directions well and is eager to please. From what I have seen, you've done a *gut* job raising him."

Relief touched her pensive expression. "I'm glad you think so. And I'm grateful Abram was there to offer advice when he broke the eggs. I was at my wit's end that night."

"It's been my experience that *kinder* who act out aren't bad," Annalise chimed in. "They're just frustrated with being misunderstood by adults." She cocked an eye toward Abram. "You were that way."

Embarrassed, Abram glanced away. "Yeah, I guess you could say I was a bit of a problem child."

Lavinia waved her hands. "Oh, let's not talk about that now. I'm ready to skate."

Samuel stood, rolling into motion. "Hurry up and get your skates on."

Laughing and teasing, everyone drifted off to join the activities. Annalise took a seat, dandling Sophie on her knee.

"You sure you don't want to give it a try?" Abram asked.

"I'm not really in the mood." She exhaled a ragged sigh. "I've got a lot on my mind."

"Oh? Anything I can help with?"

"You're too kind, Abram. But no. It's nothing. Just some unfinished business in Philadelphia." Waving a dismissive hand, she forced a smile. "It'll be fine. I—I knew it was coming, so it's not like it caught me by surprise."

Abram backed off, unwilling to press further about the matter. Maddie's business was her own. He had no right putting his nose where it didn't belong. If she wanted him to know, she'd tell him.

"Well, you still look like you could use some cheering up. A little exercise might take your mind of your problems."

Maddie gazed out at the laughing crowd. "It does look fun." Nibbling her bottom lip, she shrugged. "Why not?"

Pleased she'd changed her mind, he grinned. "Come on. Let's get you fitted with wheels."

A few minutes later, they'd both put on skates.

Wobbly, Maddie rose to her feet. "I have no idea what to do," she said, struggling not to lose her balance.

Josh skated up, skidding expertly to a stop. "Way to go, Mom!"

"Mom has a ways to go," she corrected. "This is what I get for sitting on the sidelines instead of learning."

Josh clapped. “It’s easy.” He demonstrated, pushing forward and balancing on one foot.

“Don’t think I’m ready for that just yet.”

Hiram rolled by, tagging Josh. “You’re it.” Giggling, he whipped around and rolled off.

Lavinia caught the boy by an arm, slowing him down. “Have a care,” she scolded. “Not everyone skates as well as you.”

“Place your feet apart and bend your knees a little to keep your balance.” Gliding smoothly on his own skates, Abram urged her toward the rink.

Using the rail to keep her balance, Maddie rolled forward a little. The rest of the skaters gave her thumbs-up as they sped by. “This isn’t as easy as it looks.”

Abram offered a quick lesson. “To get going, turn your foot a little and use edges of the wheels to push yourself forward.”

Maddie imitated his move, letting go of the rail and rolling forward. Her arms pinwheeled as she struggled to keep her balance.

Abram quickly slipped an arm around her waist, bracing her against a fall. The press of her weight against him caused his heart to skip a beat. An unexpected electrical connection sizzled between them.

“Careful now.”

Maddie held tight. “This is inappropriate!

What will people think of me hanging all over you like this?"

Abram righted her, getting her back on her feet. "They'll think I'm helping you learn to skate."

"I don't want to do anything that would offend anyone."

Amused, he glanced over the rim of his glasses. "Believe it or not, it's okay to be Amish and have fun." He turned to face her. "Hold my hands and I'll guide you until you get the hang of it."

"But you'll be going backward."

"I know."

She hesitated before slipping her hands into his. "Here goes."

The warmth of her palms against his sent a rush through Abram's veins. The connection was immediate, like grabbing a hot-wire fence. He never wanted to let her go.

Aware of the looks Maddie was attracting, he lifted his head and straightened his shoulders. People might think they were walking about, but he didn't care one bit. They were doing nothing to cause a scandal, and it wasn't anyone's business if he wanted to skate with a friend.

"Just follow me," he said to encourage her. "I'll do the work."

Maddie drew a steadying breath. "Okay."

Josh skated by again. "Mommy and Abram, sitting in a tree, *k-i-s-s-i-n-g*." Giggling, he took off before his mother could reprimand him.

She released a disparaging sound. "My son thinks he's a comedian."

Abram laughed and gave her a wink. "Sounds like a good idea to me."

"Abram Mueller, are you flirting with me?"

"Maybe I am. And maybe one day I'll get that kiss."

Maddie blushed clear to the roots of her hair. "I'm about as good at kissing as I am at skating. Which is to say, not at all."

"I can help you out with that," he said, and then hurried to add, "The skating, I mean." He peered over his shoulder to make sure the path was clear. "Just keep going forward, using one foot to push and rolling on the other."

Tightening her hold, she gave him a look of complete trust. "I'm counting on you not to let me fall."

He gave her hands an encouraging squeeze. "I'll be there to catch you if you do."

Chapter Nine

After an hour's skating, everyone headed to the concession stand for a break. The rink served the usual fast food: hamburgers, fries and a variety of soft drinks and other sweets.

Meal finished and skates returned, the group headed out into the parking lot. More than a few of the *youngies* were yawning as they climbed into the buggies.

Abram looked around. Because he'd ridden with his younger brother, Elam had promised to pick him up. However, there was no sign of the teenager. "Looks like Elam's forgotten he was supposed to come back and get me."

"I'll bet he got busy with his friends," Josiah Simmons said.

"The buggies are full up," Samuel said. "Though I suppose one of the boys can scoot over to make room."

"I'll give you a ride," Maddie volunteered. "It's the least I can do since you helped get my car back on the road."

"I'm all the way across town. You sure that's not too much out of your way?"

"Not at all. I'll follow your buggies."

Samuel nodded. "Sounds fine. We'll see you shortly."

Waving goodbye, Abram followed Maddie.

"Hop in, kiddo," she said to Josh.

"Okay," he muttered, climbing in.

Buckling Josh in, she opened the driver's-side door. Abram got in and buckled up. "Sorry for the inconvenience."

"Not an inconvenience at all." Maddie shifted, following the buggies out of the parking lot. Illuminated with battery-powered lights, they clipped ahead at a speed of about ten miles an hour.

"Going to take a while at this rate," she laughed, turning on her own hazard lights so a careless driver wouldn't rear-end her car on the rural roadway.

"You have to admit, the Amish aren't in any hurry to get where they are going."

She looked in her rearview. "Looks like Josh has conked out. He's been going nonstop since this morning."

"He put in a *gut* day's work. I've never known a *youngie* so eager to please."

"Going to the market has been the best therapy ever for Josh's ADHD. He's too busy and too tired to even think about acting badly," she said, keeping her eyes on the road as she guided the car. "I can't thank you enough for giving him a chance. I was afraid Mrs. Graff would get tired of his tantrums and kick us out."

"I'm happy to help."

"You've been a real godsend, Abram. I can't thank you enough for all you've done. It's gone above and beyond friendship."

Embarrassment twisted his insides. "Oh, it wasn't always that way. You haven't heard about the trouble I got into." He gingerly touched the side of his face. Even after all these years, the scar tissue felt unnatural under his fingertips. "I guess you might have wondered what happened."

Maddie focused on the road, careful to keep the vehicle's speed in pace with the buggies. "Being the mother of an overactive *kind*, I know the trouble *jungen* can get into. I'm guessing your scars happened when you were doing something you shouldn't have."

"I was a little bit more than overactive. *Out of control* would be a better phrase."

"Seriously?"

"Yes." He took a deep breath and pressed on before he lost his nerve. "And because I was a stubborn *boi* who wanted my own way, two of my friends lost their lives."

There. He'd finally said it out loud.

"I had a feeling something bad happened when you were younger. If you care to share, I'm willing to listen."

His throat momentarily squeezed shut. "I'd like to tell you," he said, forcing the words past the block. "It began when my *mamm* passed."

"Oh, Abram. I'm so sorry."

"I am afraid our *familie* fractured after *Mamm* died. At the time, I was the youngest, born after a long dry spell."

"That must have been devastating for you."

"It was. Especially since *Daed* remarried rather quickly. I hate to say it, but I didn't like my new stepmother, and she didn't like me. It felt like she was replacing my *mamm*. And then it felt like I was being replaced when more *kinder* began to come along. I was so young I really didn't understand the changes."

"I can see why you'd feel that way."

"Yeah. And Rolf was so much older than me that we weren't close."

"I'm sorry to hear that."

Clearing his throat, Abram forced himself

to continue. Very few people outside his *familie* knew the whole truth. "Noemi—that was her name—didn't like having me around and put me out of the house every chance she got. To get even, I started running with some *Englisch* boys. Anyway, when I was about ten, me and my friends got into smoking. Shane and Thomas were older, and they egged on a lot of my bad behavior."

"You smoked?"

"I wouldn't call all our coughing and hacking real smoking, but we thought we were. Stole ourselves some rolling papers and tobacco from the general store and made our own. We thought we were being cool, hanging out and being tough after school."

Maddie checked on Josh to make sure he was still asleep. Head tilted to the side, he snored softly. "That's one of the reasons I wanted to leave Philadelphia. The older kids were getting to be such a bad influence."

"One day we decided to sneak into Caleb Zook's barn. We climbed into the hayloft and turned on the little portable radio we kept hidden from our folks. Pop music was our thing. Anyway, one of the boys—Thomas, I think—rolled a couple of cigarettes and lit them. I don't remember how, but the hay caught on fire."

Her eyes widened. "Oh, no!"

Blinking against the vision forming in his mind's eye, Abram balled his hands in his lap. Mouth going bone-dry, nausea rose in the pit of his stomach. He fought back woozy sensations, making himself breathe slowly, steadily. The gentle hum of the car engine clashed with the terrible images tearing through his mind, as fast and as fierce as the fire itself.

"You know, hay burns real fast. Faster than you could ever imagine. Before we knew it, there was fire all around us. We panicked, trying to stomp it out, but it only got worse. The smoke was so thick no one could breathe. Somehow, I got out of the loft, but not before a burning post fell and hit me in the face. I was the lucky one. Shane and Thomas...they didn't make it."

"Oh, Abram. I'm so sorry you lost your friends."

He glanced out the window, letting himself disappear into blessed darkness blanketing the night. His guilt was genuine, and deeply felt. The memory of that day would never leave him. If he closed his eyes, he could still smell the odor of burning hay.

"For months, no one would talk to me or even look at me because I was that kid who killed his friends. *Daed* was so ashamed he sent me to live with Gran'pa Amos and *Maummi*."

"You were just a child," Maddie murmured. "Did your father ever forgive you?"

"No, he didn't. We weren't on good terms when he died. When I got old enough, I left Humble, thinking I didn't want to be Amish anymore. I was gone for years."

"Why did you come back?"

"I missed my *familie*. And *Englisch* life is so loud and crowded with distractions. There is traffic, televisions and phones. People are plugged in twenty-four hours a day, seven days a week. I couldn't stand all the activity. I like the peace and quiet of rural living. I like having a house without a lot of appliances to clutter it up. And I like being able to grab my fishing pole and walk down to the pond to catch my own supper."

"I'll admit city living can be tiresome," she admitted. "It's one of the reasons I wanted to come back to a rural town."

Feeling his glasses slip, Abram pulled them off and pinched at the bridge of his nose. The spectacles weren't prescription, just a pair of cheap readers from the drugstore. He'd always used them as a shield to help conceal his scars.

Now, he didn't feel the need.

Folding them up, he tucked them into his shirt pocket. Scars reminded a person not to make the same mistake. And scars were part of the healing process, turning an open wound into a sign of survival and hope.

"Most of all, I missed the church and being able to visit with the Lord. I was worried about having a nice apartment, finding a job to pay the bills and trying to juggle a social life. But it wasn't working. After twelve hours on a construction crew, all I did was go home and turn on the TV to watch some reality show I didn't really care much about."

"I haven't gone to church since I was a kid," Maddie murmured softly. "I miss it, too."

"For the longest time, I was mad at *Gott* about everything. My life was falling apart, and I couldn't see much sense in going on. One day, when I couldn't take it anymore, I walked into the nearest church and fell to my knees. And the pastor there was kind enough to show me *Gott* wasn't doing bad things to me—but that He was there for me, to lead me and comfort me through hard times. I knew then I needed to come home and make a commitment to rejoin the church and live by His word."

"I'm glad you did."

"Me, too."

By the time he'd finished his story, they'd arrived at the Muellers's property.

Maddie followed the buggies down the gravel drive and then pulled to a stop. "Home safe and sound." Shifting the car into Park, she brushed a few stray strands of hair out of her face.

Unbuckling his seat belt, Abram lingered. "Sounds like the car's running *gut*."

"It's never sounded better. Elam put a lot of work into it, I know."

"The kid's a wonder with engines. But he gets distracted when he's hanging out with his friends. Should have known he'd forget me."

"I really had a nice time tonight, and so did Josh. Thank you again for inviting us. It almost feels like we have family again."

Her words buoyed his spirits. "Would you and Josh like to come to church tomorrow? After the service, we'll be celebrating Hiram and Hershel's birthday. You're both invited."

"Would it even be allowed? We're not—"

"Before you say you're not Amish anymore, let me remind you that you *are*. It's true you are unbaptized, but neither are our *kinder*, and they are no less a part of the community. It's your heritage by birth and something you'll never lose. It's your *sohn*'s heritage, too. And unless you've been shunned and never repented, then you have as much right to sit in the pews as anyone else. If some busybody thinks you shouldn't be there, they can take it up with the bishop. Knowing James Graber, he will probably tell them the same thing."

"I'd like to. I've been going through that empty feeling you described. It's like being a hamster running in a wheel. I think I'm heading somewhere, but I'm really going nowhere. I know I've neglected the Lord, and I feel so bad for that, because I do know better."

"Coming back to the church might open up possibilities you've never considered before." Feeling a multitude of emotions crowd into his brain, he hurried on before he lost his nerve. "I think you're a fine woman, Maddie. And a great parent. And I—"

She turned to face him. Her gaze was soft, open and trusting.

Abram had so much to say but just didn't know how. Tongue tied and unable to spit the words out, he did the next best thing.

Leaning across the car's armrest, he gently cupped her cheek and kissed her.

Arriving home, Maddie pulled into the drive. Killing the engine, she sat gripping the wheel. The night had taken a turn she hadn't expected.

Abram had kissed her. Gently and sweetly.

Not once in her life had a man ever kissed her. Never. Having witnessed the violence her sister had experienced, she'd shied away from men. Those who had tried to ask her out on a date were met with a high wall of resistance.

Englisch men, she'd learned, were trouble and dangerous to know.

But what about Amish men? Taken away from her community as a *youngie*, she'd never gotten to socialize with boys raised in the faith.

Reaching up, she adjusted the rearview mirror. A glimpse into its depth revealed her shining eyes and glowing cheeks. Myriad emotions took flight. Abram's mouth on hers had felt so right. Caught in the moment, her senses had soared. The sensations flowing through her had warmed her inside.

Is this what love feels like?

She wasn't sure.

She'd never been in love before. But if she was, Abram Mueller would be the man she'd want to spend the rest of her life with. The tragedy in his past had touched her deeply. They both shared the bond of pain, loss and grief. And he had also struggled with his faith before finding the path that had led him back to *Gott* and his community.

Questions brewed. What if she rejoined the church and got baptized? That would mean she and Abram would be able to walk out together without anyone raising their brows and get to know each other on a more personal level.

She already knew she loved spending time with him and his *familie*. So did Josh. She'd missed having people of her own in her life. With only her and Josh, holidays were lonely and depressing. True, she'd made a few friends at work, as Josh had at school. But it wasn't the same as spending time with relatives.

Could she go back to being Amish?

Josh stirred behind her, murmuring sleepily. "Are we home yet, Mom?"

"We are." Maddie unlatched her seat belt and got out of the car.

Josh pawed at the buckles holding him in place. "I'll be glad when I can sit like a big kid."

Maddie's heart squeezed. Had five years really passed since she'd taken her nephew to raise? Then, he'd been a toddler, barely an armful. Now he was almost too big for her to lift. Come the end of the year, he would turn eight.

Her eyes misted. Another milestone in his life his mother would never experience. It was why she worked so hard to make sure Josh would have plenty of good memories to look back on when he was grown.

The only thing missing from the picture was a real *daed*.

As much as she did, the one thing she couldn't do was give Josh the guidance and advice a man could. A *boi* needed a father.

"Don't be growing up too fast."

Locking the car, they entered the kitchen

through the side door. Lit by a night-light, the kitchen was wreathed in shadows, as was most of the household. Most everyone had gone to bed early.

Trekking up the stairs to their loft, Maddie sent Josh into the bathroom to wash up while she turned down his bed and laid out his clothes for Sunday. The Amish dressed in their best clothes for church, and she felt the experience would be good for Josh. Though he'd had some religious instruction through school and other activities, he hadn't really been grounded in understanding and living by the word of *Gott*. Abram was right. It was time to start teaching him about his ancestry.

A few minutes later, Josh padded out of the bathroom on bare feet. Dressed in his pajamas, he hopped into bed and pulled the covers up.

"Ready for bed, sleepyhead?"

"I sure had fun tonight."

"I'm glad," she said, tucking the blankets tightly around him. Josh didn't like his feet sticking out from under the covers, fearing the imaginary monster under the bed. "And I'm proud of how you behaved this week."

A grin split his lips. "I like riding in the buggy and giving people their orders. It makes them smile. And sometimes they give me a quarter or fifty cents."

Maddie sat on the edge of his bed. "I know you weren't happy about the move to Humble."

"I was mad," he confessed, and then hurried to explain. "But I'm not anymore."

"I'm glad."

Sitting up, he threw his arms around her neck, hugging her tightly. "I—I'm sorry I stole those candy bars and broke Mrs. Graff's eggs and then yelled at her. I didn't mean to."

Touched by his gesture, she hugged him back. "I know you didn't, honey. And I'm proud of you for apologizing and making things right. That's an important step. It means you're growing up."

He let her go and lay back down. "I don't even miss my tablet or my shows anymore."

Maddie sat for a minute, mulling over her next words. She wanted to approach things carefully, making sure her motives about rejoining the Plain community were based on a true desire to reconnect with her faith and not just to please Abram.

"What would you think about being Amish?"

He brightened. "Could we?"

"It's possible. I never told you, but I was born Amish."

He nodded. "That's what Abram told me."

Her brows rose. "He did?"

"He said I could be Amish when I got bigger. If I wanted to."

"That's right." Pausing a beat, she added, "What would you think if I went back to being Amish again?"

"I think it would be neat."

"Me, too. But it would mean a lot of changes. For me…and for you. We would have to give up the car and other things. And we would have to go to church and learn about the Lord and live by His rules."

Concern puckered his forehead. "But we could still do things, like fish and skate?"

"Of course."

"And we could get a buggy and a horse and—" Excited by the idea, his thoughts sped faster than he could speak.

Maddie chuckled. "Don't go making plans yet. It's something to be taken very seriously. It's a big commitment."

He refused to be deterred. Once he grabbed on to an idea, he worried it to death like a dog with a bone. "But—but if you're Amish and Abram's Amish, you could marry him. Then I would have a dad. And you'd have someone to take care of you."

"Slow down. It doesn't quite work that way. I mean, first I would have to rejoin the church and get baptized. And then… Well, you kind of have to like someone a lot to want to marry them. And they have to like you, too."

"You like Abram, don't you?"

"I do. But I haven't known him that long. To get to know someone, you need to walk out with them."

Josh's face scrunched. "What does that mean?"

"Walking out means to get to know someone by spending time with them. It's what the Amish call dating."

"Then you should walk out with him," he announced with all seriousness.

Maddie laughed, ruffling his hair. "Let's not get ahead of ourselves," she said, leaning over to give him a kiss on the forehead. "We'll take things one day at a time. Meanwhile, you need to get to sleep. It's going to be a long day tomorrow."

"Okay," he murmured, rolling over on his side. "I'm going to think about this Amish stuff."

Giving him one final glance, Maddie left his bedside. Slipping off her shoes, she padded toward the bathroom. Her thoughts churned. She had some thinking to do, too. A lot of thinking.

Any decision she made wouldn't just affect her future. It would affect Josh's, too. Such a life-altering change wasn't to be taken lightly. And, if she was honest, she'd have to question her own motives.

Would she be returning to the church because she wanted a personal connection with the Lord—or because she wanted a relationship with Abram?

In many ways she felt torn. She missed the simplicity of her childhood and the feelings of security she'd gotten from belonging to a close-knit community. She also missed the connection she'd once felt with her savior. As a *youngie* she'd been assured *Gott* was watching over her and would bless her if she lived an obedient life dedicated to *familie* and community.

Having gotten a glimpse into the lives of the Mueller clan, she'd been given a reminder that Amish life didn't have to be as dull and drab as it was when she was growing up in Pennsylvania. New Order Amish were different. They socialized, laughed, had fun. True, there were the rules of the *Ordnung* to live by. But from what she had observed, they weren't so terribly strict.

And then there was Abram.

Suddenly flustered, Maddie felt her heart miss a beat. He had a way of looking at her that made her pulse flutter. Focused on raising Josh, she'd never given much mind to carving out a social life. She had enough problems to juggle without trying to add any sort of romance to the mix.

We're just friends.

Friends.

The word was cold. Stark.

Suddenly she felt bereft, as if cast out into the dark wilderness alone to fend for herself. She knew then the feelings she'd been trying to deny were real.

She was falling in love with Abram Mueller.

Chapter Ten

Sunday morning was clear and warm, with nary a hint of a breeze or a cloud in the sky.

Rousing Josh early, Maddie got him fed and dressed. As he scarfed down toast and scrambled eggs, she'd dressed for the day. Digging through her meager wardrobe, she pulled out one of her best dresses—a simple black frock with a modest hemline. Adding flats and hose, she pinned her hair into a bun and added a dark headscarf.

Getting Josh into the car, she headed to the morning services. Twenty minutes later, she arrived at the address Abram had given her.

Attending an Amish Sunday service wasn't quite like attending an *Englisch* church. An Amish community was divided into separate districts. Congregants living within a certain location would take turns hosting their neighbors every other Sunday. To keep things manageable, most groups were limited to about fifty persons. To accommodate the need for people to sit, the church district owned benches, which were transported to the host location and set up the evening before the event. When the weather was permissible, the services would be held outdoors. During the winter, barns or other buildings were used.

"Remember what I told you. The service will be very long, and you'll have to be quiet and listen closely. You won't understand the words, but that's okay. Just sit and listen."

"I'll be good. I promise."

Maddie pursed her lips. Josh wasn't the best at sitting through long stretches, and she hoped he'd be able to behave. She'd already made up her mind that if he started acting up, they'd leave.

As they drew closer, she saw people milling about, laughing and chatting. The men were dressed in black, which included trousers and vests that used snaps instead of buttons. Only their shirts were white. Forgoing their straw hats, they'd changed to ones made of black felt. Many of the women, however, weren't outfitted like widows in mourning. Their dresses were created from fabrics in lovely shades of blue and green. There were even some pinks and bright yellows scattered throughout. A few women wore dour black, but they were very elderly.

She tried not to stare. When she was a girl, it would have been scandalous to attend church in such bright, cheery colors. Glancing around, she recognized some of her coworkers from the market. A few curious glances raked her over. Some people offered tentative smiles and a wave to acknowledge her presence.

One clerk walked over. "*Guten morgen*, Maddie," Gretl said. "I'm glad to see you and Josh are here."

"*Ja.* Abram invited us," Maddie replied, switching to *Deitsch*.

Gretl pointed. "He's over there with his *familie*."

"*Danke.*"

Catching sight of them, Abram's face split into a wide smile. "I hope you didn't have any trouble finding the place," he said as a greeting.

"No trouble. I hope it's okay we're here."

"Of course it is. Anyone who wants to hear the word of the Lord is welcome."

Several men broke through the crowd, clapping to catch everyone's attention. "We'll be seated now," one deacon announced. "Please send your *youngies* to join Mrs. Schnabel."

"Ellen Schnabel directs the Sunday school," Abram explained, motioning for Maddie and

Josh to follow. "There are games and other activities to keep them busy while still learning their lessons. That way they don't get bored."

"I've never heard of that before. When I was a kid, we heard the same sermons as the adults."

"Three hours is a long time, so the bishop put together a separate program for the older *kinder.* When they turn thirteen, they may join the adult services."

"Sounds like a good idea."

"Bishop Graber is open to listening to the needs of his flock. The *kinder* Sunday school program has been very popular."

Spotting the other Mueller children, Josh pointed. "There they are!"

Without waiting for an answer, he dashed away to join his friends. A few of the younger women helped round the stragglers up, directing them to blankets spread out on a sunny patch of grass. Others handed out age-appropriate Bibles.

Confident Josh was in good hands, Maddie and Abram followed the directions of the deacons for the adults to be seated. As expected, the men sat on one side, the women on the other.

"I'll see you after services," Abram promised and took a seat with his brothers.

Samuel gave her a polite nod, as did Elam

and eldest brother Rolf. Gran'pa Amos turned his gaze to the ground.

Lavinia moved her daughter's diaper bag from the seat beside her. "I saved you a place."

"Come join us," Annalise invited.

Smoothing her skirt, Maddie sat and folded her hands in her lap. Shaking with anticipation, she forced herself to calm. She felt like an impostor sitting among them.

The postcard she'd received from Cash Harper weighed heavily on her mind. So did the kiss Abram had given her. If he was going to be part of their lives, he deserved to know about the issues she faced with Josh's father. As soon as she could find a moment to speak with him, she intended to confess everything. Warts and all.

Cradling her sleeping infant, Lavinia noticed her trembling. "Are you *oll recht*?"

Anxiety tightened its grip. Having made so many missteps in life, she feared the Lord had cast her aside as unworthy. "I keep expecting someone to stand up and say I don't belong here."

Annalise leaned across her sister. "You're Amish. You might have been away awhile, but the Lord will always be here to welcome you back. When we are washed in the blood of the lamb, we are saved. I believe you know that and it's why you're here today."

Maddie nodded gratefully. "*Danke.*"

The deacons walked down the rows, distributing the hymnals. Opening hers, Maddie was relieved to see the words were printed in *Englisch* as well as *Deitsch*.

"Excited?"

"Nervous."

"It'll go fast, I promise," Lavinia assured her. "The sermons will grip you with the word of *Gott*."

Conversation dropped to silence as the minister leading the group opened with a prayer, asking *Gott* to bless the day's services. He then began to lead the congregation in song.

Standing, Maddie followed along in her hymnal. The voices of the people around her blended together in perfect harmony, rising toward the clear sky in praise of the savior and His mercy toward all who accepted his precious gift of eternal salvation.

Haltingly, she joined in, Soon, she was singing with all her heart, wrapping herself in the warmth of the harmony. By the time the first chorus ended, all her tension had faded away, replaced with a feeling of belonging and acceptance.

Bible in hand, a second man stepped up to speak.

Lavinia gave a nudge. "Bishop Graber. He's the best."

A tall, angular man, the bishop looked to be in his early fifties. Setting aside his felt hat so that everyone could see his face, he began to speak in a quiet tone, forcing the congregants to lean forward to hear his words. Instead of hammering in his sermon with force, he spoke in a gentle voice.

Caught in the teachings that came directly from the Lord, Maddie's vision blurred. Blinking hard, she felt one tear, and then another, trek down her cheek. The bishop's sermon was compelling. His words, so simple, were powerful and moving.

She closed her eyes. A sense of peace settled deep inside. Sitting among the group, she basked in the unity of fellowship. Bishop Graber never missed a beat, guiding his flock with wisdom and candor.

At the strike of noon, a closing prayer brought the service to an end. Deacons collected the hymnals as the men began to stack the benches for their return to storage. The women hurried to set up tables for the luncheon. The meal would be a light one—sandwiches, drinks and homemade cake.

"A *gut* service, *ja*?" Lavinia asked as they hurried to help their hostess set up the meal.

"The best I've ever heard."

"A few people thought James Graber was too young to be bishop when Olin Wallis passed. But he was truly *Gott*'s choice to lead us."

"I liked his way of speaking very much."

"Come, lend a hand," an unfamiliar woman called. "We've got a lot of hungry people to feed."

Having attended more than one communal meal, Maddie knew what was expected.

Following the rest of the women into the kitchen, a platter of sandwiches was thrust into her hands. Speaking in *Deitsch*, a very pregnant younger woman instructed her where to take the food.

As she placed the tray on a picnic table, Gran'pa Amos walked up to her and tipped his hat. "*Gut* Sabbath."

Maddie smiled. She'd never spoken to him in more than a passing way. "*Gut* Sabbath to you, sir."

"Maddie Baum, right?"

Swallowing, she forced a nod. She could tell by the way Amos looked at her that he didn't like her.

"Ja."

"Might I have a moment of your time?"

Smoothing the wrinkles out of her dress, Maddie patted her scarf to make sure it was still pinned in place. "Of course."

"I hope you enjoyed the services," he said, removing his hat and wiping his brow. Now that it was past noon, the sun shone brightly in the sky. The heat of the day began to rise, sending people into the shade.

"Very much. I truly felt as if I were in the presence of the Lord."

"I'm glad to hear that."

"I'm thankful Abram invited us. He's been so helpful introducing Josh and me to the community."

"Abram has become very fond of you and your *sohn*."

"Your grandson has been a good friend. I feel blessed he's come into our lives."

Amos pursed his lips. A frown haunted the corner of his mouth. "By the way he speaks about you, I believe he wants to be more than *just friends*."

Maddie's nerves clenched. "And that's something that concerns you?"

"*Ja*." The elder man's expression was reserved and unsmiling. "Abram has little experience when it comes to matters of the heart. He might easily mistake his infatuation with you as something more meaningful."

"I see."

Amos shook his head. "No. I don't think you do," he said. "Abram has a chance to be chosen as a minster this afternoon. Should the Lord select him to preach the gospel, he will need a wife as deeply committed to the faith as he is."

He need not say more. The meaning behind his words was crystal clear.

"I understand," she said quietly. "Because I'm unmarried and have a child, I have a questionable character."

The old man smacked his lips, sucking at his false teeth. "I'm not trying to offend. I just want what's best for him and our *familie*. Abram has struggled to overcome difficult times and doesn't need any—um, what's the word I'm looking for—"

"Complications?"

Amos wrinkled his nose as though he smelled something terrible. "Exactly."

Maddie flinched. In the eyes of others, she was damaged goods. And hardly suitable to be a minister's wife. Or anyone's wife, for that matter.

Drawing herself up to her full height, she held up a hand. "Abram's lucky he has people who care so deeply. And I hope he finds what he's looking for in an *ehefrau*. She'll be blessed to have him. Now, if you will excuse me, I need to check on my son."

Having nothing more to say, she turned on her heel and walked away.

The day that had begun with such promise had disintegrated into ashes.

Bishop Graber's sermon had been an inspiring one. His message of love was powerful, a reminder the Lord was a living presence inside every man, woman and child. As the last notes of the final hymn had faded into the clear afternoon sky, Abram felt a surge of fresh energy in his spirit. The three-hour service had flown by in the blink of an eye. He would willingly have sat there all day.

Now and again, he'd sneaked a peek at Maddie. As the bishop spoke, her expression had revealed myriad emotions. At one point, she'd even cried, lowering her head to brush away her tears. There was no doubt in his mind that her emotions were deep and heartfelt.

Maddie Baum was a *gut* woman. And she deserved to have an *ehmann* who could take proper care of her and Josh.

He wanted to be that man.

He turned his gaze to the sky above. *If only You'll allow it, Lord.*

With the service done, the deacons and ministers gathered around Bishop Graber to join in on the meeting that would have church leaders address issues that concerned the congregation. During this time, they voted on matters that would affect the entire Plain community. Often, there would be vigorous arguments for or against something. Once every man had his say, a vote would be taken. After that, the bishop would give his reasons for approval—or why he overruled the majority.

Today, the meeting was to be an important one. Barely a month ago, Mathias Lehman had passed. A longtime minister with a fire-and-brimstone preaching style, Mathias's death had left an opening among the ministers. The deacons and remaining ministers would nominate members of the congregation who they felt should be the next to serve.

Giving the group of church elders a cursory glance, Abram rose from the bench he sat on, carrying it to a shady spot where a light lunch would be served. Homer Lipmann and his wife, Jenna, always laid out a fine spread, and he had a particular liking for Jenna's pea salad. A younger couple, they'd only been married a year. Due to give birth anytime, Jenna positively glowed with joy as she bustled around to make sure her guests were taken care of. The *youngies* would be fed first. Now and again, he caught a glimpse of Maddie as she helped bring the food out. Caught up helping move the benches, he knew it was best to stay out of the way while the women got the meal ready.

The next time he caught sight of her, she'd stepped aside to speak to Amos. He was about to walk over and join them when a hand settled on his shoulder.

"Not so fast," a familiar voice said.

Abram turned. "*Ach*, Rolf, you gave me a fright."

Rolf beamed. "Bishop Graber asked me to fetch you. The names of the men nominated for minister have been counted, and you received enough votes to be added."

"My name is among them?"

"Ja."

"I'm honored. I didn't think I would ever be worthy of consideration."

"Since you came home, you've proven yourself a good and faithful servant of the Lord. You do a lot of fine charity work in the community, and people know your heart is a *gut* one." Rolf nudged him toward the waiting group of church elders. They had assembled around a table, deep in discussion.

"If *Gott* only called men without incident in their pasts, there would be no one to preach His word," Rolf continued. "Being unworthy is exactly what makes you worthy, *bruder*. I believe you have been given a spiritual gift to guide, and that is why I—and many others—cast our lots for you."

Legs turning to rubber, Abram joined the group. The gathered deacons and ministers all greeted him with nods. Their serious expressions hammered home the gravity of the moment, for choosing a new minister was serious business.

Three other men joined the group, Liam Raber, John Beihler and Gabriel Yoder. Of the four, one would be chosen to replace Mathias. By the looks on their faces, none of the men wanted to be standing there. The chosen person would be expected to serve the church and the congregation throughout his lifetime.

Bishop Graber stepped to the head of the table. "Liam, John, Abram and Gabriel," he said, addressing the four. "Your names have been put forth by members of this congregation as candidates." He gave each man a serious look. "You all knew when you were baptized into the faith that you might someday be called to serve our Lord. Although I would hope that you would not view it as such, for some men it is a burden rather than a blessing. If you feel you cannot, for some reason, answer the call of *Gott*, then you may excuse yourself without prejudice."

Gabriel Yoder shuffled his feet. "I don't feel I am qualified."

Giving the comment due consideration, Bishop Graber scratched his bearded chin. "The issue isn't your qualifications or worthiness," he said. "The issue is your willingness. Are you willing to do the work, to reach out a hand to a soul in need? More importantly, are you willing to open your heart and let *Gott* lead you so that you may lead others?"

Gabriel nodded his assent. "If the Lord chooses me, I will answer."

The other two men also nodded.

"Aye," Liam Raber said. "I shall do the same."

"As will I," John Beihler added.

"Abram?" Bishop Graber asked.

"I, too, will accept the decision of the Lord," Abram said.

"*Gut.*" Bishop Graber motioned to one of the deacons to lay out a stack of identical hymnals.

Each man to draw looked at the prayer books. The one who found the slip of paper upon which a passage from the Bible had been written was to be the chosen. Because they were selected at random, it was believed *Gott*, not men, was making the final decision.

A hush fell. A few of the deacons and ministers lowered their heads in prayer. It was an important moment and not to be taken lightly.

"Which among you will draw first?" Bishop Graber asked.

Liam Raber stepped up. "I will," he said, and selected a book.

Gabriel Yoder selected his, as did John Beihler.

Heart thudding between anxiety and anticipation, Abram eyed the last book.

"Abram," the bishop prodded. "You gave your word that would answer *Gott*'s call."

Hand shaking more than a little, Abram bent and reached for the final book. Normally the slender volume felt light in his hands. Now it felt as heavy as a hundred-pound stone.

Each man in his turn opened their book. Each came up blank.

All eyes turned to Abram.

Drawing a breath to steady his nerves, he opened the cover of his hymnal. Inside lay a slip of paper. Written in a neat hand were the words *For not that he commendeth himself is approved, but whom the Lord commendeth.*

"The Lord has called you, Abram Mueller," Bishop Graber affirmed to the group.

Abram stared at the slip, still unable to believe he'd been chosen. "I am honored. And humbled."

The bishop motioned toward a bench. "Sit with me. We have a few things to discuss."

Giving him quiet words of encouragement, the other men drifted away to partake in lunch.

Abram sat. Closing the hymnal, he tucked the small slip of paper in his pocket.

James Graber also sat. "You look troubled."

"I don't feel it's right. Surely there are other men more deserving than me."

"*Gott* doesn't make mistakes."

"But what I did—"

"Was twenty years ago. You were a child. And while the accident was a misfortune, it was exactly that. An accident. Tragedies happen, but life does go on. It's time to stop punishing yourself and extend the hand of forgiveness to yourself."

With a dry laugh, he held out his hands and shrugged. "What will I preach about?"

"Everything you went through in your own childhood," the older man answered without missing a beat. "You can use your experiences as a tool to teach, helping other *youngies* navigate their problems. We've been needing a youth minister, and I believe you will make a difference in the lives of troubled teens in our district."

Abram's doubts lifted. Through the years, he'd felt the call to bear witness about the Lord using his past as an example, but he'd been too inhibited to share his story. Now, he felt *Gott* nudging him forward, guiding him down a new path.

"I would like that."

"I've heard you already are. Word has gotten around you are helping a new member of our community with her young *sohn*."

Abram's insides knotted all over again. "She came to town with some troubles. I've been trying to give her a hand to get back on her feet."

"I've never known you not to help anyone in need."

"She's here now." Searching through the people milling around, he saw Maddie helping the other women with their *kinder*. "That's her. Maddie Baum."

"Baum." The bishop scratched his chin. "That's an Amish name, for sure."

"Pennsylvania born. Somerset. She left before she was baptized, so she's done no wrong."

"You know, a minister is expected to marry and have a *familie*."

Abram raised his head and said plainly, "I plan to."

"It's come to my attention that you have your eye on the newcomer."

"*Ja*. I like her, very much."

"I am not one for gossip, but my wife is in the same quilting circle as Wanetta and some of the women who work in the market. They all speak highly of her."

A bit of Abram's tension eased. "I was afraid some might condemn our friendship."

Bishop Graber took off his hat, revealing a bald pate lined by thin strands of sandy hair. Heavily tanned from his hours in the sun, his skin was leathery, and his hands were callused from hard work.

"Some people might flap their jaws in disapproval, but if Maddie is sincere in her faith and wants to rejoin the church, then it's fine if you spend time in her company." He glanced over the rim of his glasses. "Provided you are chaperoned, that is."

Abram gave a short, wry laugh. "Of course. That's only proper."

"Now don't go thinking I am giving my blessing for you to get engaged. At least, not right away."

"Wasn't planning to."

"I would like to know more about her, too. If you don't mind, I plan to contact the bishop in Somerset."

"I'd have no issue with that. I doubt Maddie would, either."

"Then I'll take care of it. Won't hurt to have her records here if she ever wants to be baptized." Returning his hat to his head, James Graber stood. "Now, if you will excuse me, I'm going to go and grab some lunch. I'll see you at the ministers' meeting on Wednesday evening. We will talk a bit more about that youth program and what you'll be preaching on at the next church gathering."

"Sounds *gut*."

Then Bishop Graber walked away. Abram sat alone. A multitude of thoughts tumbled through his mind. The day had been so incredible. *Gott* had set him on a fresh path, giving him not only a destination, but a true purpose that promised a blessed life and a bright future.

A future he hoped to share with Maddie and Josh.

Chapter Eleven

Still reeling from the conversation, Maddie struggled to hold on to her composure. Though her first instinct was to grab Josh and leave, she resisted the urge. Forcing herself to be calm, she threw herself into helping the other women serve lunch and then clean up once people had finished eating.

She set to washing a pile of dishes. This helped keep her hands busy. But it did nothing to stop the recriminations from bouncing around in her head.

A wife as deeply committed to the faith as he is...

The words echoed through her mind.

News had quickly gotten around that Abram had been selected as a minister. Being chosen was a serious responsibility. Ministers were expected to serve for the rest of their life. Important figures, they also acted as role models for the rest of the congregation. It only made sense the community and his *familie* would expect him to marry a proper Amish woman.

And that isn't me.

While she was caught in her thoughts, a glass slipped from her hand, shattering on the floor. "Oh!"

Jenna Lipmann hurried to help. "Did you hurt yourself?"

Maddie glanced at her hostess, so heavily pregnant she could barely bend over. Soon, Jenna would cradle a sweet infant in her arms.

Blinking back abrupt tears, an unbidden sensation of envy rippled through her. She'd always longed for a *boppli* of her own, to experience the miracle of bringing a new soul into the world.

"No. I'm so sorry I broke it." Grabbing a dish towel, Maddie knelt to scoop up the jagged shards.

Jenna laughed, brushing off the accident with good humor. "Don't worry a bit about it. I got an entire set of those when Homer and I got married. It's easily replaced."

Another woman grabbed a broom to help sweep up the broken shards. "*Ach*, these things happen," she said, discarding the pieces in a nearby trash bin.

Feeling shaky and out of sorts, Maddie rose. A single tear trekked down her cheek, and then another.

Lavinia came to her side. "Something wrong?"

Embarrassed to be the center of attention, she shook her head. "Can't seem to pull my thoughts together."

All the women nodded in sympathy.

"Have those days myself," Annalise said knowingly. "A good, hot cup of ginger tea always helps soothe my nerves."

"And some chocolate," another woman chimed in.

The remark got a lot of laughs and some eye rolling from the other women.

Maddie offered a wan smile. "I'm just a little tired. Moving, getting settled in..."

Lavinia patted her arm. "Understandable."

"I'm sorry to make a scene. I didn't mean to ruin everyone's afternoon."

"Not at all," Jenna said. "It's why we have our Tuesday evening sewing circle. After a little Bible study, it gives us all a chance to relax and just enjoy ourselves."

"You should come," Lavinia invited, laying a hand on her arm.

"We'd love to have you," another added.

"I would love to," she said, searching for a valid excuse. "But between work and keeping up with Josh, well..." Spreading her hands, she shrugged. "No time."

"You could always drop Josh off to play with the boys," Frannie Mueller said. "Samuel keeps an eye on the *youngies* while we're out. I am sure he wouldn't mind."

"Elias and Josiah are there to help," Lavinia added. "It's not like the men don't know how to keep up with the *kinder.* They've had enough experience raising them. And Abram will help out, too, I know."

"Josh will be perfectly fine," Annalise added.

"*Danke*, I'll think about it," Maddie said, offering a compromise. It would be nice to have a circle of other women to confide in. She'd struggled raising Josh by herself and could have used the advice of other mothers to get through the difficulties raising an active young *boi*.

"*Gut*," Lavinia said, closing the matter. "You know we'd love to have you."

Kitchen cleaned, lunch ended. The women filtered back outside to join the men. Now that church was done for the day, people departed to enjoy the sunny summer afternoon.

Maddie glanced through the group, catching sight of Abram. She'd hadn't yet had a chance to speak to him. Surrounded by ministers and deacons, his attention was tied up in his new position within the church. Unwilling to disturb the men, she hoped to speak with him in the evening. Hiram and Hershel's party was scheduled for later in the day. Because she'd already promised Josh he could go, there was no graceful way to cancel.

Lavinia gave her a wave, as did Annalise.

"Party begins soon," Lavinia called.

She waved back with little enthusiasm. All the joy had been sucked out of her day.

"We'll be there."

Josh bounded up, carrying a book. "Look what I got!"

"What's that, honey?" she asked, guiding him toward the car and buckling him in his car seat.

"My study Bible." He opened the cover to a set of illustrated pages. "Today we learned about Noah and his ark."

Maddie slipped behind the wheel. "What did you think of that?"

Josh thought a moment. "I like the way Noah saved the animals from the flood," he said, nodding knowingly. "Animals are important, and we should take care of them."

"Yes, we should."

Shifting the car into gear, she followed the buggies out of the drive. The horses clopped at a steady pace. A few people smiled and waved as they passed by.

"It's a pretty big book," he said, holding the

volume in his lap. "I don't know some of the words, but Mrs. Schnabel said she would help me learn them."

"That's very nice of her."

Because he had trouble sitting still and concentrating, Josh struggled with reading. A few of his teachers had put forth the theory that he might be dyslexic, but none of his therapists had come to a conclusive diagnosis. Abram had told her Josh was eager to learn to read and count better, and she had no reason to doubt his word. Not all kids learned at the same rate in the same way.

Josh thrived when he was on his feet. Stuck behind a desk, he withered like a plant without sunlight or water. She'd hoped to enroll him in an Amish school come the fall, feeling that he would do better in a smaller classroom with more personalized attention. Memorizing dry facts and figures wasn't as important as learning the skills for a trade that would make the students valued members of the community. Perhaps when he was older, she could find an apprenticeship for him. There were always jobs for men who could work with their hands. Even Jesus Himself was a carpenter.

He closed the book, holding it on his lap. "I like Sunday school. It's neat."

"I'm glad you like it."

"We got to sing, and there were snacks and all kinds of things."

"Sounds like you had a good time."

He grinned in an exaggerated way. "Can we come back?"

Eyes going teary again, she bit her bottom lip. It wasn't fair to jerk him away from all his new friends and the routine they'd established just because she'd suffered a setback. Amos hadn't been rude, but he'd made his position crystal clear. Abram's *groossdaadi* might think she'd make an unsuitable minister's wife, but who'd said she even intended to marry him anyway?

Abram had kissed her.

Not the other way around.

Amos was wrong in thinking she'd moved to Humble looking for an *ehmann*. She hadn't. She liked being single and making her own decisions. There was no shame in being a single mom. She could still live a decent life and raise Josh in the community. Like Caesar's wife, she would have to be above reproach. And that meant cutting Abram's intentions off at the pass.

"We'll come until they tell us we can't."

"Can we go by the dollar store? I'd like to get Hiram and Hershel a present." Beaming with pride, Josh patted his pocket. "I have my own money to spend."

"Yes, we can."

"I know just what I want to get them."

"I'm proud of you for earning your own money. You're growing up so fast."

"It's fun at the Amish market. There's always something to do."

Maddie nodded. The Muellers' store was very popular in town. She liked the job and wanted to keep it. She'd just have to make it clear to Abram that it would be better if they kept things purely professional.

Conversation dropping to a lull, Josh glanced out the window, humming a new tune he'd learned.

Maddie's throat squeezed when she recognized it. The old Germanic melody was one of her *maummi*'s favorites, and she'd sung it often when Maddie was a child. Oh, how she missed those times. Even though her own community had been much more rigid and locked into tradition, her childhood hadn't been all misery and gloom.

Calming down, she took a deep breath. Tomorrow was a reset, a chance that the new day dawning would be better than the day before.

Tired of feeling lost, like an outsider staring in, she sighed. *Lord, just show me where You're leading me*, she prayed. *I'm willing to go.*

She just needed a destination.

* * *

"*Onkel* Abram, catch!" The red ball flew his way.

Snagging it with both hands, Abram tossed it to the next person in the circle. Called hot potato, the game was progressing and the rhyme that kept it going was about to end. Whoever had the ball then would be tagged out. The last person standing would be declared the winner.

The *youngies* laughed, shouting and singing the rhyme, which was silly but amusing.

The ball flew around the circle at a furious pace. By the time it came back around to him, the rhyme had ended.

"Looks like I'm out." Glad for a break, Abram tossed the ball back to the players.

"Come and eat!" Frannie called, interrupting the game.

Games coming to a pause, the *youngies* headed toward the table loaded down with the evening meal. Hiram and Hershel had asked for an old-fashioned campout, complete with tents and a cookout. The menu was simple: hot dogs to roast with all the trimmings. There would also be cake, with plenty of milk, iced tea and lemonade to drink. Earlier in the day, they'd dug a hole, circling it with stones and gathering wood for the fire that would cook the food.

Lifting his hat and giving his forehead a wipe,

Abram walked to the table. Along with buns, there was mustard, relish, ketchup, onions, chili and even sauerkraut. Side dishes included potato salad and baked beans. It was a simple meal, but a hearty one.

"My, that looks tasty."

Frannie laughed. "I'm glad the boys wanted something simple," she said. "Roasting a hot dog on a fork suits me fine."

"Looks good to me." He claimed a fork and a few franks.

"I imagine you're hungry," Frannie commented. "I didn't see you have anything for lunch."

"I was too nervous to put anything in my stomach."

"Quite a day for you," she said. "I know *Gott* will have His hand over you when you preach His word."

Feeling the weight of his new responsibility, Abram nodded. "I pray you are right. I have so much I want to say, but I want to make sure I'm preaching the Lord's words and not my own. I'll have to do a lot of studying and praying to get it right."

"Just preach from your heart. *Gott* will do the rest."

"I'll do my best."

Samuel joined them. "Come," he said to his

wife. "I'll roast us a couple and you can make them up right."

Frannie giggled. "Of course."

Abram joined the group gathered around the fire.

Maddie stood holding little Sophie while Lavinia soothed Eli, who'd accidentally lost his frank to the fire.

Pretending not to stare, Abram watched as Maddie tried to coax Sophie into taking her bottle. Gentle and patient, she spoke to the infant in a soothing tone. The expression on her face was one of sadness mingled with longing. She never hesitated to lend a hand when one of the other mothers needed help.

Sorting out Eli's problem, Lavinia claimed her child. "Thank you for watching her."

"She's such a sweet one." Maddie handed the infant over.

"I got lucky with her," Lavinia said, cradling her baby. "Even though she's teething, she's not a demanding child. Josiah is already talking about another."

Maddie glanced toward Josh. "I would love to have my—" Pausing midsentence, she shook her head.

Lavinia gave an encouraging smile. "We never know what *Gott* has planned for the future. There might yet be many blessings for more *kinder*."

A faraway look touched the depths of Maddie's gaze. "I pray you're right."

Abram smiled. He could easily imagine Maddie Baum with a houseful of *kinder*.

Giving his head a shake, he joined the two women. "I'm about to roast up a couple of franks. Would you like one?"

"I guess that would be okay."

Abram knelt, extending his long fork over the snapping flames. "How did you like church?"

"I enjoyed very it much. Bishop Graber is truly touched when he speaks the Lord's word."

He turned the franks, roasting them evenly. "I'm glad. I hope you'll come again."

"I plan to," she said. "Now that you're a minister, I'd like to hear you preach."

"It's still sinking in that I was chosen."

A pensive expression shadowed her face. "I believe *Gott* chose rightly, Abram," she said softly. "The Lord knows you have a good heart for people. You will make a wonderful minister."

Unsure what to say, he glanced away. "*Danke.*" He lifted the fork away from the fire. "I believe they're done."

"Looks delicious."

Making up their hot dogs, they each added

their favorite toppings. Abram went with onions and a nice dollop of Violet's homemade chili. Maddie was more conservative, adding only mustard and sauerkraut to hers.

He wrinkled his nose. "I didn't think anyone but Gran'pa liked that stuff."

"My *maummi* made sauerkraut in mason jars all the time. We had it with almost every meal. Cabbage was easy to grow, and it was cheap to make."

"Farm folks?"

She swallowed another bite and then wiped her mouth on a napkin. "My *opa* raised hogs. Made some of the finest bacon and ham in the state. Both my grandparents were very thrifty. They only bought what they couldn't make or trade for."

"Folks around here are that way, too."

The meal continued in companionable silence.

By the time he'd downed his second hot dog, Abram was stuffed. "Best I've ever eaten," he told his sister-in-law.

Frannie laughed. "Hope you saved room for cake."

Catching the comment, Rolf patted his stomach. "I always have room for dessert."

Disappearing into the house, Frannie returned with a double-layer German chocolate cake. Annalise followed with more paper plates and a spatula. Lavinia and Maddie cleared the leftovers, making room for the main attraction.

Everyone gathered around Hiram and Hershel.

"Happy birthday," Samuel said. "Both of you bring much joy into our lives, and we are blessed to have you."

The group launched into the traditional birthday song, singing in harmony. While Frannie served cake, the boys opened their gifts. Along with new clothes and shoes, there were a few fun things like slingshots, new fishing poles and pocketknives. Josh proudly gave each of the boys a board game and modeling clay. Nothing was expensive, and all gifts were equally welcomed. No one turned down cake, and a few even went back for seconds. Rolf even sneaked in a third piece, earning himself a deep frown from his wife.

The crowning moment of the party was the sundown hayride. Firing up his old tractor, Daniel Parsons had filled a large wagon with stacks of hay bales. To make it fun for the *youngies*, a scavenger hunt had been prepared. Small prizes had been hidden around the property for the riders to hunt up. Most everyone climbed aboard to enjoy the game. Only Gran'pa Amos declined, pleading achy old bones. Cane in hand, he limped off to retire for the evening. Through the evening, Amos had hardly spoken to anyone, preferring to keep his thoughts to himself.

"Are you coming?" Abram asked Maddie.

She shook her head. "Think I'll stay here and enjoy the fire."

Not wanting to leave her alone, Abram waved the wagon off. "We'll be here."

Daniel shifted his tractor into gear. Grinding and belching, the old thing chugged away. The *youngies* cheered with excitement. Even the adults had a smile on their faces.

"Guess we're on our own."

"Looks that way." Abram knelt, poking at the embers with a stick before throwing more wood into the pit. He'd waited all day to spend a few precious moments with her. There was so much he wanted to say.

Joining him, Maddie sat on a small camp chair, smoothing her skirt. She'd changed out of the black dress she'd worn to church, replacing it with a gray frock that fell well below her knees. Tucked under a matching scarf, not a single hair was out of place. She wore no makeup, not even a touch of mascara or lipstick.

"I've never been to a better birthday party."

"The boys are going to camp out in their tents tonight. Josh is welcome to sleep over."

"Thank you for inviting him, but I don't think he's ready for sleepovers just yet."

"Maybe some other time."

"Maybe." A long pause hung in the air. "Just so you know, tomorrow I plan to look into day care for Josh."

Surprised, he glanced up. "Oh?"

"Now that you're a minister, I know you're going have to put your attention in other directions. You don't need to be dragging my kid around with you all day."

"I don't mind. I enjoy his company." Pausing a moment, he cleared his throat. "And yours, too."

Maddie dropped her gaze. "You've already done so much. I don't want either of us to be a bother, or a burden. And I don't want it to look like I'm taking advantage."

Abram's pulse spiked. The change in her demeanor was palpable.

"Has someone said something?"

Gaze flicking away, she shook her head. "No."

"Would it have something to do with last night?" Without thinking, he reached out and took her hand. "I meant every word I said."

"I believe you."

"I know we don't know each other well," he began, attempting not to trip over his leaden tongue. "But I'd like the chance to spend more time with you and Josh. That is, if you'll let me." Even though he knew his *groossdaadi* didn't care for Maddie, he felt Amos would come around once he got to know her and Josh better.

Though a wistful smile turned up her lips, sadness lingered in the depths of her eyes. "Oh, Abram. I—"

Elam's big truck rolled up. Parking nearby, he opened the door and hopped out. A couple of his teenage buddies accompanied him.

"Sorry we're late. Got held up." He caught sight of their joined hands. A grin widened his face. "I hope we aren't interrupting anything."

Blushing, Maddie pulled her hand away and jumped to her feet. "No. Of course not." Pressing her hands to her mouth, she hurried away without looking back.

Rising, Abram took a step to follow and then stopped. A feeling deep in his gut warned him this wasn't the time to go after her.

Frustrated, he kicked the dirt beneath his feet. *If not now, when?*

Chapter Twelve

"You haven't eaten a single bite," Wanetta said, putting away the last of her dishes before wiping her hands on a dishrag. "Are you okay?"

Hands circling her cup, Maddie offered a weak smile. "I'm okay. Just feeling a little sad."

"Oh? Anything I can do to help?" Bending, Wanetta peeked inside the belly of her stove.

Maddie's stomach knotted. "I don't think anything can fix what I did."

Wanetta straightened. Dunking a tea bag into boiling water, she sat down. "I'm here to lend an ear."

"Abram Mueller kissed me."

"Is that so?"

"The night we went skating."

"If you like him and he likes you, it seems to me that might not be a bad thing. Abram Mueller's a *gut* man. You could do worse."

"But I'm not baptized."

Wanetta sipped her tea. "Let's put that aside for now. How do *you* feel about him?"

"I'm not sure. I barely know him."

The older woman cocked her head. "The heart knows what it wants. Or should I say, the heart knows *who* it wants. The hours don't matter when you've found your true love."

Maddie's composure cracked. She'd never believed in love at first sight, but that was before she'd met the shopkeeper with a gentle manner and engaging smile. Every time she was near him, her pulse kicked into high gear. It was crazy to think she'd fallen head over heels for Abram Mueller.

"Oh, Wanetta. I do have feelings for him."

"Then tell him."

"I can't. I don't know if you've heard, but Abram was chosen to replace one of the ministers who died recently."

"Mathias Lehman. He passed of cancer a month ago. And I heard the news. It's been expected for a while that Abram would be a candidate. I believe *Gott* chose rightly, and Abram will be touched by the Holy Spirit when he preaches."

"But I'm not good enough to be a minister's wife."

"Why ever not?"

"I've done some things in my life. Things that dishonor not only *Gott* but also myself."

"Everyone has skeletons in their closet. If they say they don't, they're lying. We're all human, and we all make mistakes." Wanetta reached out, patting her hand. "That's why we have the Lord to offer forgiveness. His door is always open."

Feeling a twinge behind her eyes, Maddie rubbed her fingers against her temples. Heart in agony, mind in chaos, she'd not slept a wink since Abram confessed his feelings.

"I know you're right. I have a lot praying to do."

"*Gott* will give you the answers. Just you wait and see," the older woman promised.

Finishing her tea, Maddie went to check on Josh. Having had breakfast, he was playing in the front yard with Wanetta's dog. The two frolicked in the grass, playing with a tennis ball.

Taking a seat on the veranda, a smile curved her lips, even as a pang of sadness filled her. She had a lot of thinking to do, decisions to make.

The sudden crunch of tires on asphalt shattered the peaceful morning. A sleek black sports car rolled to a stop. Parking at the curb, a man in sunglasses stepped out.

Maddie immediately bristled. Dressed in a

dark jacket, jeans and boots, the man didn't look like the sort who belonged in the neighborhood.

Lifting his sunglasses onto his head, he walked to the gate. He wore his bleached hair short and spiked. Though his eyes were evenly spaced, there was a strange crook to his nose, as if it had been broken. His jaw was sharp, and his mouth cruelly twisted.

Catching sight of her, a grin split his lips. He raised a hand and waved. "Long time, no see, Madalyn."

A chill whipped up Maddie's spine, seizing her heart with an arctic grip. Years had passed since anyone had used her given name. Recognition kicked in, flooding her with memories of violence and pain. Standing at the gate was the man she'd hoped she'd never have to lay eyes on again for the rest of her life.

The man who'd murdered her twin sister.

Cash was here. In Humble.

Rising, Maddie stepped to the edge of the veranda. Her gaze cut to Josh. Noticing the stranger, he'd stopped his play, staring curiously at the newcomer. Sensing trouble, Sully began to bark.

Don't let him scare you.

But it was hard to keep her composure when he was standing at her doorstep, ready, willing and able to cause a lot of grief. She should have known he'd track her down. When he was still behind bars, he'd made his goal to reclaim Josh perfectly clear. He'd sworn nothing would stop him.

Nothing.

"You look so surprised," he continued behind a smirk. "Didn't you get my postcard? I told you I'd be coming."

Clenching her hands, Maddie straightened her spine. No more being afraid. No more being intimidated. She had the law on her side. Until a judge ruled against her, she was Josh's legal guardian. No one in their right mind could look at Cash and believe he'd be fit to parent a small child. He had a rap sheet a mile long and was a convicted felon. Earning himself an early release for good behavior—and because prisons were overcrowded—meant nothing.

She marched down the walk, determined to cut him off. "You're not welcome here. Leave, or I'm calling the police."

Pretending she hadn't spoken, Cash opened the gate and strolled in.

"Call the cops," he said and laughed. "I'll tell them how you've been hiding my son, keeping me from contacting him. I'm pretty sure you threw away my letters and the things I sent him. My attorney kept a record, you know. He figures I have a solid case to get full custody."

Maddie held her ground. "I did it to protect Josh," she spat with contempt. "And I'd do it again."

"He's *my* son." Cash poked himself in the chest with a thumb. His voice rose, going an octave higher. "My flesh and my blood. I have rights, too. The law is on my side."

"You don't deserve to be anywhere near Josh." Lowering her voice, she made sure Josh was out of earshot. "Not after what you did to Margaret."

He returned a smirk. "I believe the court called it *involuntary* manslaughter."

Tamping down her fury, Maddie forced herself not to lash out. "There was no accident about it. It was murder."

Gaze flicking over her, Cash gave her an icy look. Though he was only in his late twenties, prison life had taken its toll. Deep lines etched his face, as did a few minor scars. The hard set of his jaw and the downward spike of his mouth gave him a mean, unwelcoming look.

"Don't cross me, Madalyn. I've done my time and had enough of people pointing fingers." His brow furrowed. "Even my own parents won't talk to me. All I've got now is my kid. I want him back."

Maddie held her ground. A shiver of foreboding sent a spray of goose bumps across her skin.

She had to keep cool, keep her wits about her. Somehow, she'd find a way to get him to leave.

"How did you even find us?"

"Your old address was on the internet," he said, giving a snarky smirk. "Public records are easy to search. It didn't take long to track you down. And a fifty-dollar bill persuaded your former landlord to tell me where your mail was being forwarded." He scanned the quiet neighborhood. "Back to Amish, eh? That should have been an easy guess. You always were Miss Goody Two-shoes, acting like you were better than the rest of us."

"Just leave us alone, Cash. Josh deserves to grow up without any more trouble in his life."

"Not a chance," he snarled. "I got no job and no place to go. With a kid, I can get public assistance. Not a bad racket, if you ask me."

Maddie gave him a look of disgust. At least she knew his true motive. Cash wanted a free ride from the government, and getting his hands on Josh would help him achieve that. Cash had always stolen what he wanted. Now he was trying to steal Josh. He didn't want his son because he loved him. He was just looking for another way to manipulate the system.

Sensing tension between the adults, Josh ran up. "Who's this, Mom?"

Smoothing his hair, Cash pasted on a wide grin. "I'm your daddy, boy." An ugly chuckle followed.

Josh looked up, confused. "Mom—"

Maddie decided the truth was the only way to handle things. She'd never told Josh about his father except to say he wasn't around. Cash's absence meant nothing, because the child didn't remember him.

"Cash is your father," she said, cringing at the fact she had voiced the words.

"I have a dad? A real dad?"

"I've waited a long time to see you." Cash knelt, opening his arms. "Come and give your old man a hug."

Shy and uncertain, Josh didn't move. "I don't know..."

Angered by his hesitation, Cash barked, "Come here, you little brat!"

"He doesn't know you!" Maddie snapped back. "Scaring him isn't going to make him love you." Doubling down, she angled her chin. "You need to leave. Now. Have your lawyer send whatever papers he wants if you think you can sue for custody. I'll see you in court. Until then, you have no right to bother us. None."

Nostrils flaring, Cash rose to his full height. His hands flexed open and shut. "You've kept my kid away from me for years," he snarled. "No more. I'm taking my son. Today."

Upset by the arguing, Sully set to barking harder, lunging forward in a protective stance. Drawn out by the commotion in her front yard, Wanetta stepped out onto the veranda. "Settle down, Sully." Seeing the stranger, she set her hands on her hips. "What's going on here?"

"It's nothing, Mrs. Graff," Maddie called. "Just talking to an old acquaintance."

Sully barked harder before settling into a long, threatening growl.

Lifting his T-shirt, Cash reached into the waistband of his jeans. A dark metal object appeared in his hand. He pointed his gun at the dog. Irritation made his voice high and shrill. "Call off your mutt or I'll kill it!"

Chilled by the sight of the weapon, Maddie moved to protect Josh. "Cash—no!"

Sully lunged. The dog latched on to the intruder's leg, burying his fangs deep in vulnerable skin.

Desperate to escape the attack, Cash kicked out. "Get away!" he cried, firing off a wild shot. The blast of the bullet ricocheted through the quiet neighborhood.

"Sully, get away!" Wanetta cried, terrified.

Cash kicked a second time. His steel-toed boot connected with the dog's chest. Yelping in pain, the big shepherd backed off.

Furious and injured, Cash aimed the gun

straight at Maddie. "Get out of my way or I swear I'll put a bullet in you!" His cold, deliberate threat came out as a snarl.

"No!" Driven by the instinct to protect her nephew, she dashed toward him without thinking. Hands circling his arm, she attempted to deflect the angle of the gun away from the innocent bystanders. But Cash Harper was bigger than she was. Stronger. All she had to fight with was a hundred pounds of sheer determination.

It wasn't enough.

A gush of air ejected past Cash's lips. "You ain't got what it takes!" Wrenching his arm free, he slammed the butt of the gun against her temple.

Struck hard, Maddie staggered back, dropping to the ground. The world around her tilted and reeled. Time went completely out of focus. Struggling to remain conscious, she fought against the darkness sweeping around her, cocooning her in an airless void.

Pressing a hand against the injury, she tried to rise. Dizziness assailed her from all sides. With an inner strength she didn't know existed, she clung to alertness. "Don't," she gasped. "Please, don't hurt him..."

Her pleas meant nothing.

Stepping around her, Cash snatched Josh off his feet. The child kicked and screamed, but he was no match for a fully grown man.

"Mom!" he wailed. "Mooooommy—"

Dashing away, Cash shoved his son into the front seat of his car. Racing around, he slid behind the wheel. Gunning the engine, he sped off.

Just like that, Josh was gone.

Lulled by the sway of the buggy, Abram yawned, struggling to keep his eyes open. He hadn't slept a wink the night before, tossing and turning in his bed.

An elbow nudged him in the side. "You awake?"

Lids snapping wide, he nodded. "I'm here," he said, rubbing tired lids with two fingers. Hat perched at a jaunty angle, Gran'pa Amos offered a cheery grin. "Early bird gets the worm, minister."

"That's what they say."

Amos gave the reins a little flip. "You look like you have something on your mind. What's troubling you?"

Abram shook his head. "I am still wondering why the Lord called me."

"You've been walking the right path since you came back to Humble and got baptized. You still have a bit of *Englisch* about you, but it doesn't seem to bother people."

"I know you think I've gone a bit too modern with the store."

"I admit I didn't like the idea of using computers or hiring *Englisch* employees, but when I look at the numbers, I can see the market is growing and making a profit. That benefits not only our *familie*, but those who work for us, too."

"The world is changing. And we have to change with it or be left behind."

Fortunately, Bishop Graber had a good head on his shoulders and would often approve the use of implements that would improve the health and well-being of the community, and that included economically. The use of cell phones was becoming more common, and the devices were permitted to be used for business or emergency purposes.

As Abram viewed it, there was a difference between using and abusing a privilege. In his mind, being obedient to his maker kept a man on the right path.

"*Ach*, I agree. But it doesn't mean we have to entirely abandon our ways or give in to the push of technology."

"We don't have to give in, so much as adapt. The *Ordnung* isn't carved in stone. Bishop Graber has been generous on what conveniences can and can't be used. People seem satisfied with his judgment and have benefited."

"The *youngies* coming up have so many

things to distract them now. They want cell phones, vehicles and other things that pull them away from the community."

"That's why I want to work with teens who are questioning staying Amish," Abram explained. "I want to show them they still fit in without needing those things."

"If anyone knows that struggle, it is you. Just lean on the Lord and He will guide your steps."

"I'm praying hard for patience and wisdom."

Amos gave him another nudge. "Now we just need to get you married. A minister needs the support of a *gut* wife."

Abram glanced up. "The bishop mentioned that."

"Oh?"

Sucking in a breath, he nodded. "We talked a bit about my intentions toward Maddie."

Amos stiffened, keeping his eyes on the road ahead. His hands gripped the reins a little tighter, causing the horse to snort from the sudden tension. "And what did he say?"

"He said as long as she is sincere in her faith and desire to rejoin the community that he didn't see any reason why I couldn't walk out with her."

"Are you serious?"

"Calm down. I'm not planning to marry her tomorrow. Part of dating is getting to know someone. I like Maddie and her *sohn*. And I'd like to find out if they'd fit into my life."

"But she's—"

"What?"

"She's got a *youngie*!" Amos spat.

"Yes, she does. And I won't condemn her because some sweet-talking fellow stole her heart. No *kind* is ever a mistake, no matter the circumstances."

"It's not the same," Amos countered through a sigh of frustration. "She's not one of us."

"Are we not to welcome strangers as the Lord has welcomed us?"

"*Och*, that's true. But please, promise me you won't let your feelings for Maddie lead you down the wrong path."

"How many times do we have to have this conversation? You think I'd break my commitment to the church?"

"I'm afraid you might be tempted. And that would tear our *familie* apart." Amos looked at him, his gaze deeply serious. "You would go under the *bann*."

A mix of emotions twisted Abram's insides. "When I came home and got baptized, I pledged to live by *Gott*'s commandments. I would never betray that sacred vow. When I marry—*if* I marry—my wife will be an Amish woman. Does that satisfy you?"

Bringing the buggy to a halt at an intersection that led to a main thoroughfare into town, his *groossdaadi* shifted uncomfortably. "I pray you are strong enough to keep your word."

He had no chance to reply. The shrill wail of emergency sirens cut through the air, deafening in their intensity. Approaching fast, a couple of sheriff's vehicles and an ambulance raced across the asphalt at top speed, disappearing as quickly as they'd appeared.

"*Ach*," Amos murmured. "Accident somewhere in town."

Abram nodded. Most accidents in Humble involved buggies and gas-powered vehicles. *Englisch* drivers were bad about not making allowances for slower, horse-drawn conveyances.

Amos nodded toward the dash. "Turn on the radio and see if there's any word."

Abram snapped on the dial. More than a convenience, the radio offered a way to keep up with local news and events, especially in the case of emergencies. Because it was battery powered, Amos hadn't squawked too loudly when he'd installed it.

A news flash in progress cut through the static. "Local authorities are responding to a call involving a domestic dispute with a possible kidnapping," the newscaster announced. "Early this morning, a male subject stormed a local boardinghouse…" The live news broadcast continued, revealing more details.

"That's Wanetta Graff's place."

Blood pressure spiking, Abram forced himself to calm. Now he realized the emergency vehicles had been heading toward Maddie's neighborhood. As far as he was aware, she was the only boarder with a child.

Unknown male. Kidnapping.

Rubbing his temple, bile rose from the pit of his stomach. The one thing Maddie rarely mentioned was Josh's father. The details he'd picked up were sketchy. Everything about her suddenly made sense.

Maddie Baum was a woman on the run.

Abram had a feeling what she was fleeing—*whom* she was fleeing—had finally caught up with her.

Feeling helpless, his hands curled into fists. "We need to find out if everyone is okay."

Amos gave him a sharp glance. "It's not our place. We should let the police handle this."

"Maddie has no one. It doesn't matter if she's Amish or *Englisch.* Can we not be kind enough to lend our support?"

Amos heaved a sigh. "I suppose… For the sake of being decent." Catching a break in the traffic, he gave the horse a smart tap with the reins, guiding the buggy into a turn. The horse's hooves clattered on the asphalt with a steady *clop-clop* as the beast picked up the pace.

Abram held on tight. Made for distance and not for speed, the ride was bumpy and uncomfortable. The miles disappeared beneath its hooves.

Twenty minutes later, Amos guided the buggy down the tree-lined street that would take them to their destination.

Gazing ahead, Abram's heart froze. Lights flashing, the police vehicles and ambulance they'd seen earlier surrounded the boardinghouse. A local news van was also on the scene. A man with a mike in one hand was being videoed by a cameraman, broadcasting the breaking news across the airwaves. Though the hour was early, there was a group of people who lived in the neighborhood gathered on the sidewalk.

Amos gasped, engaging the brake that would halt the buggy's progress. The horse snorted with displeasure but obeyed.

Abram abandoned his seat. His feet had no more than touched the ground before he sprinted off. After he passed curious onlookers, a couple of officers halted his progress at the perimeter of the property.

Looking past them, he saw Wanetta standing with a uniformed man and a couple of other lawmen he didn't recognize. Locked in the backyard, her mongrel hound howled to be set free.

Anxiety ripped through him, chilling his senses. His gaze roamed, taking in every detail. The police vehicles gathered around were a rare sight in Humble.

He sent up a silent prayer. *Lord, let everyone be under Your hand.*

"What's happened?"

The deputy guarding the perimeter eyed his plain clothes. "Who are you?"

"Wanetta's a friend," he explained. "And one of her boarders works at my market. Maddie Baum. She has a *kind*, a little *boi*. Josh."

Eyes hidden behind impenetrable sunglasses, the deputy attempted to direct him away from the scene. "Domestic dispute," he explained in a clipped tone. "Story we're getting is some guy pistol-whipped his ex and kidnapped the kid."

Chapter Thirteen

Numb from shock, Maddie sat quietly on the sofa in the parlor. An EMT gingerly probed the ugly bruise marring one side of her face.

"Looks like you might have a mild concussion," the man said. "Are you sure you don't want to go to the hospital?"

Wincing under the painful probing, Maddie shook her head. "I'm fine. Really. Thank you." Though shaky, her voice was firm.

The EMT backed off, picking up his bag. "I don't think it's bad. If you feel sluggish or confused, it's okay to rest. Just make sure someone's with you for the next twenty-four hours."

"I understand."

The EMT nodded. "Sounds good." Picking up his bag, he turned to the sheriff standing nearby. "You can talk to her now."

A tall man in uniform stepped up. "I'm Sheriff Ward. Based on the details Mrs. Graff gave us, we have a description of the suspect and the vehicle he was driving. Do you have any idea where he might be heading?"

Maddie's insides turned to painful knots. A terrible ache thudded behind her temples. Confused and unsettled, everything around her felt blurry and out of reach, as if she was trapped in the depths of a nightmare from which she couldn't awaken.

Burying her head in her hands, she searched her beleaguered brain, trying to remember the few pieces she knew about Cash Harper. "All I know is he's from California and might have family in Sacramento."

"That's not much, but it's something," Ward said, jotting a few notes on a small pad. "Mrs. Graff got part of the plate, too. The sooner you tell me what's going on, the sooner we can find your son."

Maddie lowered her hands, preparing to answer. She caught a glimpse of Wanetta hovering at the parlor entryway. Hat in hand, Abram Mueller stood nearby.

"The paramedic said we could come in," her landlady explained.

Sheriff Ward waved them in. "Come on in, folks. I'm sure Miss Baum would appreciate the support."

"How are you, dear?"

Fighting to keep her focus, Maddie tentatively probed the lump on the side of her temple. "A little headache, but I'll be okay."

Face etched with concern, Abram's gaze raked her. "We came as soon as we heard the news on the radio."

Heart missing a beat, Maddie forced herself to swallow past the lump building in the back of her throat. "Had a little accident this morning."

"Sounds more like assault to me."

Sheriff Ward held out a hand to calm his concern. "I'm getting the details now."

"The EMT said she could have something to drink," Wanetta said, nervously wringing her hands. "I can make tea."

"Sounds fine," Ward said.

"Is there anything you need me to do?" Abram asked.

Maddie blinked hard to keep her tears at bay. Cry now, and she'd fall to pieces.

"Could you pray for Josh's safe return?"

Abram looked to the sheriff. "May I?"

Ward gave a brisk nod. "Of course."

Crossing the room, Abram knelt beside the sofa. He held out his hands. "Please."

Feeling self-conscious, Maddie shyly offered her hands. His fingers closed over hers, offering a strong embrace.

Closing his eyes, Abram bowed his head. "Dear Lord, we come to You in prayer to protect Josh from his abductor, a man who would prey on the vulnerable. Please lay a hand of protection over him and return him safely. In Your precious name we pray. Amen."

Listening to his heartfelt words, Maddie felt a sense of security emanate through her aching body. She added her own plea. "Please, *Gott*, don't let Cash hurt him."

"I know the Lord is listening. Put your trust in Him and He will see you through." Abram gave her hands a little squeeze. "I'm here. Anything you need, just ask."

"Danke."

Wanetta returned. "Tea's on." Setting a tray on the coffee table, she handed around mugs filled with steaming black tea. "There's one for you, too, Sheriff."

"Don't mind if I do."

Maddie gratefully accepted a mug, wrapping cold hands around the warm ceramic. Her mind spun in all directions. She just couldn't seem to get focused.

The sheriff cleared his throat. "I know this is difficult, but I need to know everything about the man who took your son."

Abram rose. "We should leave so you can talk."

Maddie shook her head. What she had to say wouldn't be easy, but it was necessary. All the lies she'd told had finally caught up with her, and Josh was paying the price. It was time to tell the truth. She could only hope Abram and the rest of the community wouldn't condemn her for deceiving them. Her nephew's safety—maybe even his life—depended on total and complete honesty.

"I'd like it if you'd all stay. I want everyone to know the truth. The whole truth."

"Any time you're ready to begin."

"First, I need to tell you Josh isn't my son. He is my nephew." Before anyone could react, she drew a fortifying breath and blurted, "Five years ago, I took him to raise after Cash murdered my twin sister, Margaret."

Ward's brows shot up. "Is that so?"

"Yes. They fought all the time, and Cash was violent with her. After Josh was born, he got even worse. He didn't want to support a new baby. When Margaret decided she'd had enough, she was going to try for sole custody of Josh. Knowing he was going to lose her for good, Cash freaked out."

"What did he do?"

Maddie momentarily glanced away, focusing on the commotion outside. The arrival of the ambulance and police cars had unleashed a tirade of unwelcome images, dragging her back to the day her sister died.

"He broke into her apartment and attacked her while she was sleeping."

Wanetta gasped. "How terrible!"

"Margaret tried to get away, but Cash was bigger than she was. He hit her until she was unconscious. The ambulance took her to the hospital, but something was wrong. She went into a coma and died three days later."

"And he only got five years in prison?" Sheriff Ward asked.

"Yes. That's it. He pleaded down to involuntary manslaughter to avoid a jury trial." Throat aching, she sucked in a breath. Unwelcome tears blurred her vision. "A few months ago, I got a notification that Cash was going to be paroled. Through the years he'd written letters, threatening to take Josh away from me when he got out of prison. I panicked. I didn't have the money to hire an attorney. I thought if I moved, I could keep him from finding us until I could save enough to fight him in court."

"What an awful thing to go through," Abram murmured.

"Margaret was barely sixteen when she met Cash. She thought she was in love with him. But he was wild and mean. I never trusted him. Not for one minute."

"I understand why you wanted to keep Josh away from his father," Sheriff Ward said. "And while I don't condone hiding a child from his parent, I see why you wanted to avoid Mr. Harper. He's obviously holding a grudge. You're lucky he didn't hurt you as badly as he did your sister."

A headache kicked behind Maddie's temples. Guilt, fear and anger hammered her from all sides. She knew what Cash Harper was capable of when he felt cornered and threatened—he'd destroy everyone and everything in his path.

Violently and without remorse.

"It wasn't me I was worried about."

Sheriff Ward stood, adjusting the angle of his hat. "A BOLO—be on the lookout—has been issued throughout the county. We know he's armed and dangerous, so we're prepared for trouble."

"I know you're doing your best, Sheriff. But what will happen to Josh if you can't find him?" Calm breaking, a single tear slid down her cheek and then another. She angrily wiped them away. The unthinkable hovered in the back of her mind like a voracious beast ready to snatch away all hope. "What if he's gone forever?"

Another half hour passed before things settled down.

Finishing the interview, Sheriff Ward had

headed out to join his deputies. All emergency personnel were on high alert, as were the citizens. Humble was a small community, and word had gotten around that a child was in danger.

Unwilling to leave Maddie alone, Abram kept his seat. Though she'd told him her twin had died suddenly, she'd never gone into details. The narrative she'd shared was chilling.

Gazing at her, he saw her entire body tremble with emotion. Mug clutched between her hands, she remained unmoving on the love seat. Sunlight filtering through the curtains in the parlor lit her pallid complexion. The bruise on her face was swollen, turning to a shade of purple. The violence with which she had been attacked both shocked and disturbed him. He never would have guessed that such danger lurked in her past.

Face etched with worry, Wanetta hovered nearby. "You're so pale, dear. Could I get you something to eat?"

Maddie shook her head. "I'm not hungry." Her words simmered with fright and weariness.

"You need to keep up your strength."

"I couldn't. My stomach is in knots. I'm so afraid of what Cash might do to Josh. Will he feed him, keep him warm?" Her words broke off in a fresh sob.

Bursting into tears, Wanetta sobbed, too. Her

hands flew to her mouth. "Oh, dear… This is entirely too much for my nerves. I've never known such trouble." Hurrying away, she returned to the haven of her kitchen. Pots rattling, she set to keeping herself occupied with her cooking.

Expression going blank, Maddie stared straight ahead. Arms wrapped around her body, she rocked back and forth, as if to comfort herself. Suddenly, she broke down sobbing.

Looking at her, so solitary and alone, Abram longed to draw her close and reassure her that everything would be all right. Frustration simmered beneath his calm.

"We are all praying *Gott* will keep Josh safe and get him home as soon as possible."

Scrubbing her hands across her bruised face, she shivered. Her feelings of helplessness and hopelessness were apparent.

"I'm sorry. Faith isn't something I have a lot of right now," she said in a defeated tone. "I think I've given up on *Gott*. I prayed He would protect Josh from Cash, and look what's happened. What if Cash hurts him to get even with me? He's mentally unbalanced. He'd do something like that."

Panicked and fearful, she was in desperate need of healing and peace. In her mind, she couldn't comprehend why a loving savior would allow such a terrible thing to happen to her child.

"*Gott* has no control over the bad things in this world. Humans are full of sin and do evil every day. And being a believer in the Lord doesn't mean you won't suffer when that evil comes to your doorstep."

"Then why believe? Why have any faith at all?"

"Because believing means knowing *Gott* will be there to see you through when your days are at their darkest. The Lord warns that we will have tribulations. Not if, but when. And faith means knowing He will hold us close as we walk through the gloom and lead us back to light."

She slowly lifted her gaze. Tears glistened along the edges of her eyes. "*Danke*," she whispered. "You're going to make a fine minister."

"We're all lifting you and Josh up in prayer. Whatever the outcome, know it will be what *Gott* intends."

"I know in my heart what you're saying is true." Pressing her hands together, Maddie briefly touched her lips with the tips of her fingers. "Trying to keep Josh safe—I strayed so far from the Lord. I thought I could handle things. Truth is, I messed up."

"You did the best you could. If I were in your

place, I can't say I wouldn't have done the same thing."

She glanced toward the kitchen. "I feel horrible. I've bought such trouble to Wanetta's door. I'd hoped Cash wouldn't find us. I was a fool."

Abram searched her face. Looking at her, he saw a woman fighting to start a new life in an unfamiliar place with limited resources. The one thing he didn't see was a woman who gave up easily. She'd left everything she knew behind, taking every cent she had to pack up and come to Wisconsin. She was doing it by herself and with a young child in tow. More than hope, that took strength and determination.

A knock at the parlor door interrupted. A man dressed in a suit peered into the room.

"Excuse me, Miss Baum. My name is Brian Wolfe, and I'm a reporter with WYOU news. If you feel up to it, I'd like to do a brief interview about the man who murdered your sister."

Eyes widening, Maddie paled. "No, I couldn't. I have nothing to say about that horrible man."

The newsman persisted. "We'd like to make it our lead story on this evening's broadcast."

Abram rose, cutting him off. "I think that's enough." Stepping forward, he took the man's elbow and turned him around. "You should leave."

Guiding the unwelcome intruder through the

living room, he opened the front door and propelled the newsman onto the veranda.

The man huffed, jerking away. "Well, I never... I thought the Amish were peaceful."

"We are. Until we're riled up. The Bible doesn't say we have to put up with any nonsense."

The newsman turned, gesturing to the nearby cameraman by slicing a single finger across his throat. "She doesn't want to talk." Microphone in hand, he headed across the yard. "Let's see if we can get a few remarks from the neighbors. They ought to have a few things to say about trouble in their neighborhood."

The cameraman nodded, following in the anchorman's wake. "Got it."

Abram watched the men go. Though he understood the press had a place in society, he didn't care for the predatory ways of the media. The Amish did not take photographs, nor did they really welcome outsiders taking them. But given the proliferation of cell phones and other means of capturing images, the intrusion of the camera's lens was inevitable. The *Ordnung* allowed photographs or video as long as it was obvious they weren't seeking to draw attention to themselves.

There had been a time when he'd been in a similar place, facing the scrutiny of the police, the press and the community. People wanted to know what had happened and why. For a ten-year-old, it was frightening and overwhelming. Fortunately, he'd had the support of his *familie* to help him through. Maddie had no one.

Having taken a seat under the shaded awning, Amos watched the men go. "I don't care for *Englischers* like that," he remarked with distaste.

Abram took the opposite seat, setting his hat on a small table between them. "They have a job to do. They'll get the word out that a *youngie* is missing."

Amos angled his head, giving him a sideways glance. "How's the girl?"

"Maddie. Her name is Maddie. And she's a nervous wreck. Can't say I wouldn't be the same."

"I overheard a couple of the deputies talking." Amos ran a hand through his thick beard. "Is it true Josh isn't her *sohn*?"

"Josh belongs to her *schwester*. Maddie took her nephew to raise when her twin was attacked and killed by his father."

"She's a twin?"

"*Ja*. Josh was too young to remember his real *mamm*, so she's raised him as her own."

"I never would have thought..." Remorse darkened the elderly man's face. "I am ashamed I spoke to her so harshly."

"What are you talking about?"

"Yesterday after the service, I had a few words with her."

Abram stiffened. "I see."

"What I said about her character was unkind and uncalled-for. I didn't know the *youngie* wasn't hers."

Abram searched his elder's face. Given their earlier conversation, it wasn't hard to guess what Amos might have said. Now he knew why Maddie had been so reserved and withdrawn at Hiram and Hershel's birthday party. And why she'd rushed away without giving him an answer.

"I understand you felt the need to say your piece. But it wasn't your place."

Amos shrugged helplessly. "I was just looking out for your reputation. You're a minister now."

"I'm also a man. And I'm well able to make my own decision about who I'd like to walk out with. The only one that should be concerned is Bishop Graber. He'd be the one who'd have the final say as to whether or not Maddie was suited to be a part of our community."

"I just thought—" Growing angry, the old man stamped his foot. "Our *familie* has a reputation in this town. A *gut* one."

Abram peered over the rim of his glasses. If

his *groossdaadi* had any flaw, it was his tendency to be tactless and blunt. Unless someone had the courage to call him out, he refused to budge from his point of view.

"Your arrogance gets the better of you. And so does your pride. You are being stubborn and foolish over something that's probably never going to happen. *Gott* commands us not to judge others for the path they have chosen."

"But she *did* tell a lie," Amos pointed out, trying to justify his position. "That was dishonest. And *Gott* doesn't bless the deceitful."

"Maddie did what she felt was right. Knowing what she's been through, I can't say I blame her. And I doubt a loving *Gott* would punish a woman for trying to protect her own blood kin from a violent felon."

Brought up short, the old man's anger fizzled away. Embarrassment reddened his face. "Forgive me for being a fool."

Abram sighed heavily. He wasn't angry. But he was deeply hurt. He hadn't even gotten to step up to bat before striking out.

"What's done is done."

"I didn't mean to do wrong." Eyes tearing, the old man's bottom lip trembled. "I was just thinking that if you got married, I'd be left on my own."

Abram felt a sudden rush of sympathy. "Did you really believe you'd be abandoned?"

Amos slowly nodded. "Aye. I guess I did. I've gotten used to having you around the house."

"Oh, Gran'pa. You know none of us would ever leave you on your own. If I were to marry, there would always be a place for you in my home. You know that."

"Never wanted to be stuck away in a *dawdy haus*," the old man grumbled, regaining his sass.

Abram shook his head. "No chance of that ever happening. But it doesn't matter. The way it's going, there's no wife in my future."

"Perhaps I should speak to her," Amos offered, hurrying to repair the rift.

"Just leave it be. She has enough on her mind." Brushing his hair out of his eyes, Abram reached for his hat. The day was growing warmer as the morning progressed. Time had slipped by, edging toward noon.

Now that the emergency vehicles and news van had departed, the onlookers drawn by the excitement also drifted away. Only a single deputy remained. Presumably he was guarding the house and keeping watch in case the fugitive doubled back. The gun on his hip was ready to be drawn.

Though the use of firearms was permitted for hunting, the idea of raising a weapon toward another human being went firmly against his beliefs. The Bible taught that members of the Amish community were not to return evil for evil. Their lives were based on their faith. And their faith taught them to let the Lord fight their battles.

"We should go. The police don't need us getting in the way."

Grunting more than a little, Amos hefted his weight out of the chair. "What are you going to do?"

Abram held up a hand to cut the sun. "I'm going to pray the Lord brings Josh home safe."

Chapter Fourteen

Unable to rest because of the terrible images racing through her mind, Maddie sat staring at Josh's empty bed. Though it was neatly made up, his toys were still scattered atop it.

Exactly where he'd left them.

She reached out, picking up one of his favorite toy trucks. Raising him on her own had been tough, but she'd loved every minute. Losing him felt like someone had chopped off her arms and legs. She'd been a part of his life since the moment he'd taken his first breath. Margaret, so young and foolish, hadn't been ready for the demands of an infant. When her sister shirked the duties of motherhood, she'd stepped in.

Barely seventeen when she had the baby, Margaret had been more interested in her hairstyles and makeup. And the more she flounced around, the more Cash seethed.

Returning the toy to its place, she shook her head. After Margaret's death, she'd glossed over her twin's shortcomings. Truth be told, her sister had had no business having a *youngie*. Josh was the actual victim—another thing for his immature parents to battle over.

A knock at the door offered a welcome distraction.

"Maddie?" Wanetta called, twisting the knob and peering inside the loft. "Are you there?"

"I'm here." Wiping her eyes with a handful of wadded tissues, she stood and brushed a few wrinkles out of her dress.

Tray in hand, Wanetta crossed to the kitchenette. "I made a fresh batch of chicken soup. Thought you might like some." Setting out a bowl, she lifted the lid keeping it warm. "There's corn cakes with honey butter, too."

When she glanced at the food, Maddie's stomach churned. The most she'd managed was a cup of peppermint tea. The only thing keeping her on her feet was raw nerves and fear.

"I'm not hungry."

Straightening, Wanetta gave her a look. "When's the last time you washed up?"

Maddie glanced down at her dress. It was the same one she'd had on when Josh was taken. "I don't remember." Changing clothes, brushing her teeth... She'd done none of that. All she could do was stare at Josh's empty bed. He'd been missing over forty-eight hours.

A burst of fresh tears racked her. Through the agonizing days, she'd cried, worried and fretted herself into a complete frazzle. Guilt tore at her like vultures over a carcass, ripping away pieces of her soul.

Wanetta took her by the shoulders. "You just sit down and get off your feet a minute."

Dabbing her eyes, Maddie sat. "I'm sorry for all the trouble, Wanetta."

"No trouble at all. You need to look after yourself, keep your strength up. Josh will need his *mamm* when he comes home."

"I'm not—"

Wanetta silenced her. "Pshaw! Of course you are. Any woman that nurtures a *youngie* is a *mutter*. Don't ever think less of yourself because you didn't birth him."

"I was afraid people wouldn't understand."

"Don't listen to what others have to say. The only judgment that matters is that of our Lord. And he'd never frown on you for taking that *boi* on to raise." Reaching out, she offered a reassuring pat. "You are a courageous and strong *fraulein*. Don't ever forget that."

"*Danke*," she murmured. Despite the encouraging words, she still felt inadequate and hopeless.

"Bishop Graber stopped by earlier. There will

be a gathering at the community center to pray for Josh. Do you feel well enough to go?"

Maddie looked around the loft. When she'd first viewed the rental, the attic space had felt huge. Now it felt tiny. Closed and claustrophobic. Like the walls were shrinking, boxing her in from all sides. Depression had ground her down to dust, suffocating her with unrelenting pressure.

She needed to get out. Get away. If she spent another hour inside, she'd go mad.

"I would like that."

Wanetta eyed her unkempt appearance. "Why don't you go clean up? Once you're dressed, I'll help you put up your hair. The bishop is sending a car. The driver will be here at six."

"I appreciate his kindness." She started to rise. "I'll get ready."

Wanetta sat her down again. "First, eat."

Reaching for a spoon, she tried a bit. Swimming with chicken and vegetables, the soup was delicious. Within minutes, she'd eaten the entire bowl.

"I'll tidy things while you wash up."

Grateful for the help, Maddie headed into the bathroom. Twenty minutes later, she was clean from head to toe. Choosing a plain gray dress, she paired it with a pair of dark hose and black flats.

Leaving the loft, Maddie went downstairs. As promised, Wanetta waited to help with her hair. Combing out the damp strands, the older woman created a single braid and then wound it up into a tight bun. "*Ach*, if only you had a *kapp*, you'd look like a proper Amish woman," she commented, using bobby pins to hold the style in place.

"I haven't worn one since I was a girl. Can't imagine doing it now."

Wanetta's mouth formed an O. "Are you not going to rejoin the church?"

Maddie suddenly felt overwhelmed. All the dreams she'd woven about returning to the Amish community had disintegrated. Her life and her newfound faith had been turned upside down. Seeds of doubt and despair had planted themselves deep. Instead of plucking them, she'd allowed them to take root and fester.

We reap what we sow.

She'd deceived the people who were supposed to be her friends. Worse, she'd put the entire community in danger by attracting the likes of a convicted felon with a dangerous agenda. Humble was a quiet community. Its residents were peaceful, eschewing violence. They had no way to defend themselves against a mentally unstable fugitive.

"I don't think so. I don't think I'll even want to stay in Humble if the police don't..."

The bishop's driver knocked at the door. "Is everyone ready?"

"Time to go." Wanetta threw a dark cloak around her shoulders. "Josh will come home, dear. I know the Lord is watching over him."

Attempting to regain her composure, Maddie brushed her hands across her face. Following the driver to the car, she slid into the back seat. Bible in hand, Wanetta sat beside her.

"Lot of traffic tonight," the driver commented, navigating down a street lined with buggies.

Maddie glanced out the window at the gathering crowd. By the looks of it, most of them were Amish. Bishop James Graber was there, as were several of her coworkers from the market. Abram and his relatives were there, too. Most every member of his family was present.

She gasped. "So many people."

"You're one of us," Wanetta said in a reassuring voice. "And the Amish take care of their own."

"But I lied to everyone."

"I know it might seem hard to believe, but you've been forgiven. And by the Lord's grace, you will be saved. Accept Him into your heart. The Lord will do the rest."

Her doubts began to lift. She'd been fearful *Gott* would punish her for her deceptions.

But instead of pushing her away, the Lord had folded her in His loving embrace, surrounding her with people who could guide her steps back to her faith.

All she had to do was say yes.

The driver parked near the entrance of the building. Unhooking her seat belt, Maddie stepped out of the van. Wanetta followed.

Lavinia rushed to meet her, pulling her into a tight embrace. "How worried you must be."

Annalise, too, gave her a hug. "We've been praying day and night for Josh's safe return."

Samuel gave her hand an encouraging squeeze. Rolf offered a smile and a nod.

Only old Amos kept his distance, unable to look her in the eyes.

Abram came last. "How are you?"

Conflicted, Maddie stood like a deer caught in the headlights. She'd never forget that he had been the first to come the day Josh was kidnapped. But he hadn't come again since that day. "Trying to hold it all together."

"I've been wanting to see you," he said, leaning in so only she could hear. "But I wasn't sure if you would want to see me. I know what my gran'pa said, and he owes you an apology. He had no right to speak to you that way."

Pursing her lips, Maddie stepped back. "I don't want to cause trouble in your *familie*. I understand why Amos said what he did. *Gott* has called you to the ministry, and you don't need any distractions from the likes of me."

"Maddie, I—"

An awkward silence stretched between them.

James Graber hurried up, greeting her with a solemn expression. "Maddie, I am sorry I didn't get to speak with you at last Sunday's services. I always try to welcome newcomers personally."

Grateful for the interruption, she offered a smile. "*Danke* for arranging this prayer meeting."

"The Bible says whatever we bind on earth shall be bound in heaven. *Gott* is there for those who gather in His name." Hand at her elbow, the bishop guided her toward the front of the crowd. "I'd like you to open with a brief statement. After that, I will lead the opening prayer. Abram, too, would like to speak. I hope that's all right."

Stomach clenching at the idea of standing in front of so many pairs of eyes, Maddie pressed a hand to her middle. "Of course."

Out of the corner of her eye, she caught sight of the local news van. The broadcaster was preparing to go live when the shrill blast of sirens shattered the calm. People gasped as the sheriff's SUV turned in to the parking lot and rolled to a stop. A state police unit followed closely behind.

Panicked, Maddie's blood pressure dropped

to zero. Numbness crept through her, locking her in place. Had something terrible happened? Why else would the police zoom in with lights and sirens on?

Her pulse pounded in her ears, deafening her. *Please...* Her mind spun with a thousand horrible scenarios. What if Cash had harmed Josh?

Onlookers watched anxiously as Sheriff Ward exited his vehicle. Walking around, he opened the passenger door. A woman in a nurse's uniform stepped onto the pavement. Bending, she reached inside. A figure wrapped in a blanket appeared.

Catching sight of a shock of brown hair, Maddie's eyes widened. Recognition filtered in.

"Josh!"

Screaming his name, she broke free of her paralysis. Rushing to him, she swept him up in a bear hug. "Thank *Gott* you're safe!"

"Mom!" Wriggling out of the blanket, Josh hugged her back.

The crowd burst into cheers.

Untangling herself from his grasp, Maddie looked him over. Hair matted and face stained, his clothes were a wrinkled mess. Unsure whether to laugh or cry, she did both.

"Are you okay?"

"I think so." Sniffling, Josh wiped his runny nose.

Accompanied by a state trooper, Sheriff Ward

stepped up. "We got him. Mr. Harper is on his way to jail as we speak."

"Tell me everything. Please."

Smiling broadly, Ward tipped back his hat. "You can thank Josh for getting himself free. Mr. Harper cuffed him and locked him in a hotel bathroom while he went to buy supplies. Josh managed to slip out of them and get away. The clerk at the front desk called 911."

Josh thrust out his arms. "My wrists are real skinny. I twisted until I could get them off."

Concern puckered her brow. "Did he hurt you?"

Josh went silent for a moment and then shook his head. "No. I was scared at first, but I pretended I liked him. He gave me candy and sodas and said he'd take care of me 'cause he was my dad." Frowning, he shook his head. "He's not my dad. I don't like him." He touched his mouth, raw and red. "He put tape over my mouth so I wouldn't yell when I got scared."

Horrified by the trauma Cash had inflicted on his own child, goose bumps blanketed Maddie's skin. She couldn't begin to imagine how terrified Josh must have been to be taken away and restrained by a strange man.

Eager to talk, Josh tugged at her arm. "That man tried to tell me you weren't my mom. But

I didn't believe him." He gave her an imploring look. "You'll always be my mom, right?"

She hugged him again. "Always and forever."

Sheriff Ward crossed his arms with smug satisfaction. "I can guarantee you Mr. Harper won't bother anyone again. Not only did he break the conditions of his parole, but he'll also face charges for auto theft, assault and kidnapping. He's also wanted for a string of robberies in other states that funded his travels. By the time the judge gets finished, he'll sit behind bars for a long time."

Maddie pressed a shaky hand to her brow. The threat Cash had cast over their lives was gone, evaporating like fog under the rays of the rising sun.

There would be no more running. No more hiding. No more lies.

"Can I take him home?"

The sheriff nodded. "You can. We had a nurse check him out, and he seems to be okay. There's a few details we'll need to wrap up on your side, but those can wait a few days."

Heaving a sigh, she took Josh's smaller hand in hers. Closing her eyes, she made a silent promise. *I'll keep my eyes on You from now on, Lord.* She now had no doubt as to the power of *Gott*'s grace and glory.

Hope for the future filled her.

Opening her eyes, she caught a glimpse of Abram. Hat in hand, he stood on the periphery. Noticing her notice him, he gave her a tentative smile. Their gazes locked.

Pulse jumping, her emotions crested on a wave of longing. Heart jumping to her throat, oxygen drizzled from her lungs.

Turning away, she forced herself to tamp her feelings down. Abram was a friend. That was all. *Gott* had called him to the ministry. They walked two different paths now. Even though she loved him—and believed he loved her—she had to let him go.

The moment he'd heard Josh had been taken, Abram had begun to pray. Fervently and without ceasing. The image of the *boi* being ripped from his mother's arms had haunted him. It made no difference that Josh was Maddie's nephew and not her natural-born child. She'd cared for the *boi* since he was a toddler, loving and raising him as her own. She was his *mamm*, and no one blamed her for doing what she'd felt would keep Josh safe.

"Thank You, Lord, for answered prayers."

Standing near his shoulder, his *groossdaadi* added, "Amen."

Abram glanced at his elder. "I know you didn't

think much of Maddie, but I hope you see how wrong you were. She's a *gut* woman."

"I see," Amos admitted. "And I've asked *Gott* to free me of my arrogance and bind my tongue from speaking hurtful words. If I could take back what I said, I would."

"What's done is done." Abram resettled his hat on his head. "I heard the sheriff say Maddie could take Josh home. We should go."

The old man gave him a nudge. "Why don't you offer her a ride?"

"I don't think she wants to see much of me right now."

Amos clucked his tongue. "I saw how she looked at you earlier. And I see how you look at her. If ever two people belonged together, it's you two." He gave another nudge. "Go."

"You think she would have me?"

"Only the Lord knows what He has planned for your future," the old man said. "It's time for you to find out."

Lavinia gave an encouraging nod. "I know she's the one," she said, grinning.

"*Ach*, she would make a fine sister-in-law," Samuel added, giving him a thumbs-up. "Just don't blow it."

Rolf rolled his eyes. "More *kinder* on the way, for sure."

Abram felt heat creep through his face. "Don't start counting our *boppli* just yet."

Amos leaned against his cane. "Oh, you'll be *verheiratet* soon enough." Laughing, he offered a sly wink. "And then you'll be saying how henpecked you are."

"I think I'd kind of like being henpecked. Matter of fact, I'm looking forward to it. Someday..."

At least, that's what he hoped.

Having waved in the newsmen, Sheriff Ward was speaking with the anchor. Maddie had given a few brief remarks, thanking everyone for their prayers of support. Excited by the attention, Josh waved to the cameras.

Abram stood at the periphery, waiting until the cameras had stopped rolling. Wrapping up the segment, the newsmen cleared out. Bishop Graber, too, took his leave, encouraging Maddie to come again to Sunday services.

Catching a chance to speak to her, Abram took his hat off. Fingering the brim, he walked up.

Josh immediately broke away from his mother, running to greet him.

"I'm so glad to see you!"

Kneeling, he embraced Josh. "I missed you, too. I am so happy the Lord bought you back safely."

Josh pulled away, his face serious. "I didn't

like that man. He can't be a dad. Dads don't do mean things like that."

"No," he said softly. "A real man doesn't do mean things."

"I want *you* to be my dad!" Josh blurted.

Abram's brows rose. "Really?"

"Yeah, 'cause you do things with me and don't get mad when I mess up."

"I don't recall you've messed up anything," he said gently.

"I did. Remember? I stole that chocolate. And then I broke Mrs. Graff's eggs. But you didn't get mad. That man. He yelled at me. A lot. He said I'd listen to him or else." Still deeply affected by the experience, a shiver tore through his body.

Abram stood and set his hands on Josh's shoulders. "Don't be afraid. *Gott* will look after you and your *mamm*." He raised his gaze to Maddie's, finishing softly, "And so will I."

Still a bit teary, Maddie wiped at her eyes. "You've always been so kind, to both of us."

"Everything turned out the way the Lord meant it to."

"I'm just relieved Cash will be going back to prison. Everything I'd feared would happen, it's not there anymore. It's like all the gloom and doom has been wiped out of our lives."

"The Lord has a powerful hand. When He wants a path cleared, he'll clear it."

"I believe it," she said, smiling.

"Then I hope that means you're thinking about staying."

Casting a glance toward Amos, her expression crumpled. "I'm not sure. I want to, but..."

Abram hurried to make amends. "Gran'pa knows he was wrong. He had no right to speak to you the way he did, and he's sorry."

"It's okay. I understand where he was coming from. And I forgive him. I just hope you can forgive me."

"You never owed me any explanations. I was willing to take you at face value. I still am."

"What do you mean?"

Anxiety twisting his stomach, he blew out a breath. "Well, you never gave me an answer the night I asked about being a part of your life."

Pressing a hand to her mouth, Maddie sniffed. "I guess I do owe you an answer."

He held out his hands. "It's okay if you think it's too quick. I know you and Josh have been through a lot. And we haven't known each other long. But I'll be honest. I fell in love with you the day we met."

Maddie glanced at Josh and then back to him. "I'm just not ready. Not yet. Maybe never. I just don't know."

Abram's confidence shriveled. "I can respect that."

Drawing a breath, she added, "But I'm not saying no."

"You're not?"

Lips trembling, her gaze brightened. "I like you. A lot. You could even say I'm falling in love with you."

Pulse kicking up a notch, hope stirred. "You are?"

"I think so." Lashes fluttering, her cheeks took on a blush. "But I don't want to rush into anything. I need a little time." She gave him a shy, hopeful look. "If that's okay..."

A grin spread across his face.

"The Lord only gives us one day at a time. I'm willing to wait until you're ready for more." Reaching for her hand, he circled her small, delicate fingers with his own larger ones. From now on, he intended to be by her side. Protecting her. Loving her. "I'll be there. I promise."

She squeezed back. "I'd like that."

"Could I start by giving you a ride? That is, if you don't mind going in a buggy."

Maddie cocked her head. "I don't mind at all." She reached for Josh's hand. "Let's go home."

Steps in sync, they all walked together.

Tipping his head, Abram lifted his gaze toward the clear evening sky. The sun setting on the horizon painted the endless space with slashes of pinks, blues and purples. The sight was as breathtaking and beautiful as the woman walking beside him. As they passed by, Gran'pa Amos lifted his hat and nodded his approval.

He nodded back. The Lord had indeed answered his prayers. The day that had begun with such uncertainty had ended with perfect peace.

As for tomorrow…

Tomorrow was the first day of the rest of their lives.

A smile curved his lips. "Amen," he murmured. "Amen."

Epilogue

One year later

"Oh, Maddie, you look beautiful."

Blushing, Maddie brushed her hands over the soft fabric of her simple Amish frock. She'd labored over it for months, choosing the material, cutting the pattern and sewing every stitch by hand. She'd chosen the soft peach shade specifically because it complemented her complexion and brought out the blue in her eyes. A white apron and a pretty pair of flat sandals completed the look.

"Are you sure?"

Lavinia grinned. "I've never seen a prettier bride."

Standing behind her, Annalise held up the final touch. "Let me help you pin your *kapp* on and we're all done."

Standing still, Maddie clasped her hands. She'd grown her hair long, and it stretched to her waist. "It has been so long since I've worn one."

"You're one of us now," Lavinia said, her laugh rippling with merriment.

"Better get used to it," Annalise said, winding up the long strands and pinning the stiff white *kapp* into place with bobby pins. "No backing out. You're baptized now."

Maddie made a last nervous check in the mirror. She hardly recognized the woman staring back at her.

Over the last year, her life had transformed in ways she'd never dreamed of. She'd arrived in Humble on the run from a dangerous felon. Abram and so many others had extended the hand of friendship, offering a safe harbor. And Josh's behavioral problems had all but vanished. He had plenty of friends, and he loved the teachers at his new school. He'd also continued to spend time with Abram, working at the market. The two were practically joined at the hip.

Once she'd decided to settle permanently in Wisconsin, she'd consulted with Bishop Graber. Dedicating herself to the church meant she would have to take classes to reacquaint herself with the traditions and expectations of the Plain community. The bishop also wanted to make sure she was sincere in her commitment to her faith. Having acquired her records from the Somerset community, he was able to affirm the details about her mother's own shunning. He'd reassured her what had happened when she was a *youngie* wasn't her fault, and that she shouldn't blame herself for her *mamm*'s choices.

At times, she'd struggled, questioning her motivation and doubting her choices. Bishop Graber had patiently counseled her, pointing her to Scripture that would answer her questions and ease her mind. After spending many hours in study and prayer, she knew in her spirit she'd been called back. Returning to the Amish was the right decision. For her. And for Josh.

She'd believed her baptism would be the happiest day of her life.

She was wrong.

The happiest day of her life was when Abram had gotten down on one knee and proposed. In front of *Gott* and everyone, he'd declared his intention to the entire congregation to make her his wife.

Everyone had applauded.

And she'd said yes.

Wanetta poked her head into the dressing room. "It's time."

Nervous, Maddie pressed a hand to her stomach. "I guess this is it."

"Mrs. Abram Mueller," Annalise said, eyes sparkling. "I love the sound of it."

Lavinia embraced her. "I am so happy to have a new *schwester*."

Wanetta wiped at her eyes. "It's almost like I'm marrying off my own daughter."

Maddie gave her a quick hug. "Thank you for hosting us."

"My pleasure, dear. Now, get yourself out there and marry that man."

"Yes, ma'am."

Heading through the parlor, Maddie walked into the backyard. An entire month had gone into the preparations for the big day. The decorations were tastefully arranged, with swaths of fresh flowers and a simple but elegant bower. Most everyone in the community had been invited, and the place was filled to the brim with friends and coworkers alike.

Though she'd felt bad resigning from the market, she could no longer do work that required the use of a computer. Her days of living *Englisch* were over. Abram had assured her she'd have quite enough on her hands putting together their new home. After he'd proposed, they'd decided not to build a house. Instead they would live with Gran'pa Amos and remodel the old structure, modernizing it with new propane appliances and adding on additional rooms. Generations of Muellers—past, present and future—would all come together under one roof.

Seeing her, the guests broke into song. Every voice joined in perfect harmony for the hymn opening the ceremony. The "*Das Loblied*," or "*Hymn of Praise*," was sung in *Deitsch*.

Bible in hand, James Graber waited to perform the nuptials. Dressed in his Sunday best, Abram stood to his left. Squirming with anxiety, Josh, too, waited beside him. Hair a little longer, he was dressed in a suit like those the other boys his age wore.

Catching sight of them, tears blurred Maddie's vision. A complete and perfect peace filled her heart. Brushing away the moisture, she walked up to join them, standing to the right of the bishop. Annalise and Lavinia walked with her, standing nearby.

Josh beamed. "Oh, Mom. You look so pretty."

Maddie smiled back. "Thank you, honey."

She was so proud of him. Shooting up like a weed, Josh was close to turning nine. The trauma of the kidnapping had initially frightened and confused him. It had taken several months in counseling to help him process all that had occurred. Josh now knew she wasn't his birth mother. But that didn't make their bond any less close or meaningful. In his mind, she was his *mamm*. And that's all that counted.

As for Margaret, it was time to let her rest in peace. She hoped her twin was looking down from Heaven and smiling.

I'll take care of your baby, she thought, glancing up into the clear blue sky.

Josh was thrilled, too, that Abram was joining their *familie*. Their little duo was about to become a trio. He couldn't be happier Abram would be his very own *daed*.

Reaching for her hands, Abram grinned from ear to ear. His grip was firm and reassuring. "I knew from the day I met you that I'd marry you."

Tipping her head, Maddie focused on his face. A sensation of warmth and security circled her heart. He was so tall and so strong. And handsome.

"I knew from the day I met you I'd say yes." Her voice, a little husky, was filled with pure emotion. In a few minutes, they would both solemnly promise to love and bear and be patient with each other. Nor would they separate from each other until *Gott* parted them through death. And then they would be wed in holy matrimony, joined by the Heavenly Father who had brought them together. Then they would walk through this world together. As a minister's wife, she'd stand by his side to serve the church and their community. Together, their faith would grow deeper and stronger.

Thank You, dear Lord, for sending me Your best.

Basking in the glow of the sunshine and the joy filling her, she'd never felt such peace. Her lonely struggle had ended. *Gott* had truly blessed her, leading her to a place she could call home.

Forever.

* * * * *

Dear Reader,

Welcome to Humble, Wisconsin! I hope you enjoyed meeting Maddie Baum and Abram Mueller, the couple who kicks off the first book set in this idyllic New Order Amish community.

Both Maddie and Abram have secrets that keep them from moving forward with their lives. Though Abram comes from a large, boisterous Amish family, his growth into his faith was hindered by a difficult childhood and a terrible accident that left him physically scarred. The death of Maddie's twin sister holds her back from forming any meaningful relationships. She's also lost touch with her faith. Thanks to Abram's friendship, she is able to overcome her fear and let go of the past that haunts her.

Those of you who read my debut, *The Cowboy's Amish Haven*, might be wondering why I didn't write another Texas Amish Brides book. Well, I wrote this book first. But I never could get the opening quite right. So I set the manuscript aside to work on a new project. When I sold that book to Love Inspired, it was a dream come true. It also gave me the inspiration to go back and rewrite the first book. Much to my surprise, it sold, too! So, hang tight. More books are on the way! Abram's younger sister,

Lavinia, will have a story of her own soon. And Rebecca Schroder's story is also in the works.

As always, I love hearing from readers. If you'd like to keep up with my future releases, sign up for my blog and/or newsletter at www.pameladesmondwright.com. If you prefer snail mail, I can be reached at PO Box 165, Texico, NM 88135-0165.

Sending many blessings!
Pamela

Get 4 FREE REWARDS!

We'll send you 2 FREE Books plus 2 FREE Mystery Gifts.

Both the **Love Inspired®** and **Love Inspired® Suspense** series feature compelling novels filled with inspirational romance, faith, forgiveness, and hope.

YES! Please send me 2 FREE novels from the Love Inspired or Love Inspired Suspense series and my 2 FREE gifts (gifts are worth about $10 retail). After receiving them, if I don't wish to receive any more books, I can return the shipping statement marked "cancel." If I don't cancel, I will receive 6 brand-new Love Inspired Larger-Print books or Love Inspired Suspense Larger-Print books every month and be billed just $5.99 each in the U.S. or $6.24 each in Canada. That is a savings of at least 17% off the cover price. It's quite a bargain! Shipping and handling is just 50¢ per book in the U.S. and $1.25 per book in Canada.* I understand that accepting the 2 free books and gifts places me under no obligation to buy anything. I can always return a shipment and cancel at any time. The free books and gifts are mine to keep no matter what I decide.

Choose one: ☐ **Love Inspired Larger-Print** (122/322 IDN GNWC) ☐ **Love Inspired Suspense Larger-Print** (107/307 IDN GNWN)

Name (please print)

Address Apt. #

City State/Province Zip/Postal Code

Email: Please check this box ☐ if you would like to receive newsletters and promotional emails from Harlequin Enterprises ULC and its affiliates. You can unsubscribe anytime.

Mail to the **Harlequin Reader Service:**
IN U.S.A.: P.O. Box 1341, Buffalo, NY 14240-8531
IN CANADA: P.O. Box 603, Fort Erie, Ontario L2A 5X3

Want to try 2 free books from another series? Call 1-800-873-8635 or visit www.ReaderService.com.

*Terms and prices subject to change without notice. Prices do not include sales taxes, which will be charged (if applicable) based on your state or country of residence. Canadian residents will be charged applicable taxes. Offer not valid in Quebec. This offer is limited to one order per household. Books received may not be as shown. Not valid for current subscribers to the Love Inspired or Love Inspired Suspense series. All orders subject to approval. Credit or debit balances in a customer's account(s) may be offset by any other outstanding balance owed by or to the customer. Please allow 4 to 6 weeks for delivery. Offer available while quantities last.

Your Privacy—Your information is being collected by Harlequin Enterprises ULC, operating as Harlequin Reader Service. For a complete summary of the information we collect, how we use this information and to whom it is disclosed, please visit our privacy notice located at corporate.harlequin.com/privacy-notice. From time to time we may also exchange your personal information with reputable third parties. If you wish to opt out of this sharing of your personal information, please visit readerservice.com/consumerschoice or call 1-800-873-8635. **Notice to California Residents**—Under California law, you have specific rights to control and access your data. For more information on these rights and how to exercise them, visit corporate.harlequin.com/california-privacy.

LIRLIS22

Get 4 FREE REWARDS!

We'll send you 2 FREE Books plus 2 FREE Mystery Gifts.

Both the **Harlequin® Special Edition** and **Harlequin® Heartwarming™** series feature compelling novels filled with stories of love and strength where the bonds of friendship, family and community unite.

YES! Please send me 2 FREE novels from the Harlequin Special Edition or Harlequin Heartwarming series and my 2 FREE gifts (gifts are worth about $10 retail). After receiving them, if I don't wish to receive any more books, I can return the shipping statement marked "cancel." If I don't cancel, I will receive 6 brand-new Harlequin Special Edition books every month and be billed just $4.99 each in the U.S or $5.74 each in Canada, a savings of at least 17% off the cover price or 4 brand-new Harlequin Heartwarming Larger-Print books every month and be billed just $5.74 each in the U.S. or $6.24 each in Canada, a savings of at least 21% off the cover price. It's quite a bargain! Shipping and handling is just 50¢ per book in the U.S. and $1.25 per book in Canada.* I understand that accepting the 2 free books and gifts places me under no obligation to buy anything. I can always return a shipment and cancel at any time. The free books and gifts are mine to keep no matter what I decide.

Choose one: ☐ **Harlequin Special Edition** (235/335 HDN GNMP) ☐ **Harlequin Heartwarming Larger-Print** (161/361 HDN GNPZ)

Name (please print)

Address Apt. #

City State/Province Zip/Postal Code

Email: Please check this box ☐ if you would like to receive newsletters and promotional emails from Harlequin Enterprises ULC and its affiliates. You can unsubscribe anytime.

Mail to the **Harlequin Reader Service:**
IN U.S.A.: P.O. Box 1341, Buffalo, NY 14240-8531
IN CANADA: P.O. Box 603, Fort Erie, Ontario L2A 5X3

Want to try 2 free books from another series? Call 1-800-873-8635 or visit www.ReaderService.com.

*Terms and prices subject to change without notice. Prices do not include sales taxes, which will be charged (if applicable) based on your state or country of residence. Canadian residents will be charged applicable taxes. Offer not valid in Quebec. This offer is limited to one order per household. Books received may not be as shown. Not valid for current subscribers to the Harlequin Special Edition or Harlequin Heartwarming series. All orders subject to approval. Credit or debit balances in a customer's account(s) may be offset by any other outstanding balance owed by or to the customer. Please allow 4 to 6 weeks for delivery. Offer available while quantities last.

Your Privacy—Your information is being collected by Harlequin Enterprises ULC, operating as Harlequin Reader Service. For a complete summary of the information we collect, how we use this information and to whom it is disclosed, please visit our privacy notice located at corporate.harlequin.com/privacy-notice. From time to time we may also exchange your personal information with reputable third parties. If you wish to opt out of this sharing of your personal information, please visit readerservice.com/consumerschoice or call 1-800-873-8635. **Notice to California Residents**—Under California law, you have specific rights to control and access your data. For more information on these rights and how to exercise them, visit corporate.harlequin.com/california-privacy.

HSEHW22

COUNTRY LEGACY COLLECTION

Cowboys, adventure and romance await you in this new collection! Enjoy superb reading all year long with books by bestselling authors like Diana Palmer, Sasha Summers and Marie Ferrarella!

YES! Please send me the **Country Legacy Collection**! This collection begins with 3 FREE books and 2 FREE gifts in the first shipment. Along with my 3 free books, I'll also get 3 more books from the **Country Legacy Collection**, which I may either return and owe nothing or keep for the low price of $24.60 U.S./$28.12 CDN each plus $2.99 U.S./$7.49 CDN for shipping and handling per shipment*. If I decide to continue, about once a month for 8 months, I will get 6 or 7 more books but will only pay for 4. That means 2 or 3 books in every shipment will be FREE! If I decide to keep the entire collection, I'll have paid for only 32 books because 19 are FREE! I understand that accepting the 3 free books and gifts places me under no obligation to buy anything. I can always return a shipment and cancel at any time. My free books and gifts are mine to keep no matter what I decide.

☐ 275 HCK 1939 ☐ 475 HCK 1939

Name (please print)

Address Apt. #

City State/Province Zip/Postal Code

Mail to the **Harlequin Reader Service:**
IN U.S.A.: P.O. Box 1341, Buffalo, NY 14240-8571
IN CANADA: P.O. Box 603, Fort Erie, Ontario L2A 5X3

*Terms and prices subject to change without notice. Prices do not include sales taxes, which will be charged (if applicable) based on your state or country of residence. Canadian residents will be charged applicable taxes. Offer not valid in Quebec. All orders subject to approval. Credit or debit balances in a customer's account(s) may be offset by any other outstanding balance owed by or to the customer. Please allow 3 to 4 weeks for delivery. Offer available while quantities last. © 2021 Harlequin Enterprises ULC. ® and ™ are trademarks owned by Harlequin Enterprises ULC.

Your Privacy—Your information is being collected by Harlequin Enterprises ULC, operating as Harlequin Reader Service. To see how we collect and use this information visit https://corporate.harlequin.com/privacy-notice. From time to time we may also exchange your personal information with reputable third parties. If you wish to opt out of this sharing of your personal information, please visit www.readerservice.com/consumerschoice or call 1-800-873-8635. Notice to California Residents—Under California law, you have specific rights to control and access your data. For more information visit https://corporate.harlequin.com/california-privacy.

50BOOKCL22

COMING NEXT MONTH FROM **Love Inspired**

IN LOVE WITH THE AMISH NANNY
by Rebecca Kertz

Still grieving her fiancé's death, Katie Mast is not interested in finding a new husband—even if the matchmaker believes widower Micah Bontrager and his three children are perfect for her. But when Katie agrees to nanny the little ones, could this arrangement lead to a life—and love—she never thought could exist again?

THEIR MAKE-BELIEVE MATCH
by Jackie Stef

Irrepressible Sadie Stolzfus refuses to wed someone who doesn't understand her. To avoid an arranged marriage, she finds the perfect pretend beau in handsome but heartbroken Isaac Hostettler. Spending time with Sadie helps Isaac avoid matchmaking pressure—and handle a difficult loss. But can they really be sure their convenient courtship isn't the real thing?

THE COWBOY'S JOURNEY HOME
K-9 Companions • by Linda Goodnight

Medically discharged from the military, Yates Trudeau and his ex-military dog, Justice, return to the family ranch vowing to make amends—and keep his prognosis hidden. Only civilian life means facing reporter Laurel Maxwell, the woman he left behind but never forgot. When she learns the truth, will she risk her heart for an uncertain future?

CLAIMING HER TEXAS FAMILY
Cowboys of Diamondback Ranch • by Jolene Navarro

After her marriage publicly falls apart, single mom Abigail Dixon has nowhere to go—except to the family she thinks abandoned her as a child. Not ready to confront the past, Abigail keeps her identity a secret from everyone but handsome sheriff Hudson Menchaca. Can he reunite a broken family...without losing his heart?

THE SECRET BETWEEN THEM
Widow's Peak Creek • by Susanne Dietze

In her mother's hometown, Harper Price is sure she'll finally learn about the grandfather and father she never knew. But that means working with local lawyer and single dad Joel Morgan. Winning his and his daughter's trust is Harper's first challenge...but not her last as her quest reveals shocking truths.

EMBRACING HIS PAST
by Christina Miller

Stunned to learn he has an adult son, widower Harrison Mitchell uproots his life and moves to Natchez, Mississippi, to find him. But Harrison's hit with another surprise: his new boss, Anise Armstrong, is his son's adoptive mother. Now he must prove he deserves to be a father...and possibly a husband.

LOOK FOR THESE AND OTHER LOVE INSPIRED BOOKS WHEREVER BOOKS ARE SOLD, INCLUDING MOST BOOKSTORES, SUPERMARKETS, DISCOUNT STORES AND DRUGSTORES.

LICNM0622

Visit ReaderService.com Today!

As a valued member of the Harlequin Reader Service, you'll find these benefits and more at ReaderService.com:

- Try 2 free books from any series
- Access risk-free special offers
- View your account history & manage payments
- Browse the latest Bonus Bucks catalog

Don't miss out!

If you want to stay up-to-date on the latest at the Harlequin Reader Service and enjoy more content, make sure you've signed up for our monthly News & Notes email newsletter. Sign up online at ReaderService.com or by calling Customer Service at 1-800-873-8635.

RS20